PULP Literature

PULP LITERATURE PRESS
Issue No. 13, Winter 2017

Pulp Literature Press, Publisher
Jennifer Landels, Managing Editor
Melanie Anastasiou, Acquisitions Editor
Katherine Howard, Assistant Editor
Daniel Cowper, Poetry Editor
Amanda Bidnall, Copy Editor
Mary Rykov, Proofreader
Claire Milne, Graphic Designer
Anat Rabkin, Mathemagician
Rachel Kuo, Advertising Co-ordinator
Susan Pieters, Consulting Editor

Cover painting, *The Shadow*, by Zoran Pekovic. Illustrations for 'It Rained Then' by Anat Rabkin. Illustrations for *Allaigna's Song: Aria* by JM Landels. All other illustrations by Mel Anastasiou.

Pulp Literature: ISSN 2292-2164 (Print), ISSN 2292-2172 (Online), Issue No. 13, Winter 2017.

Published quarterly by Pulp Literature Press, 8540 Elsmore Road, Richmond BC, Canada V7C 2A1, pulpliterature.com at $15.00 per copy. Annual subscription $50.00 in Canada, $66.00 continental USA, $82.00 elsewhere. Printed in Victoria BC, Canada by First Choice Books / Victoria Bindery. Copyright © 2017 Pulp Literature Press.

Pulp Literature Press gratefully acknowledges the support of the Canada Council for the Arts.

Canada Council Conseil des arts
for the Arts   du Canada

Pulp Literature is a proud member of the Magazine Association of BC.

TABLE OF CONTENTS

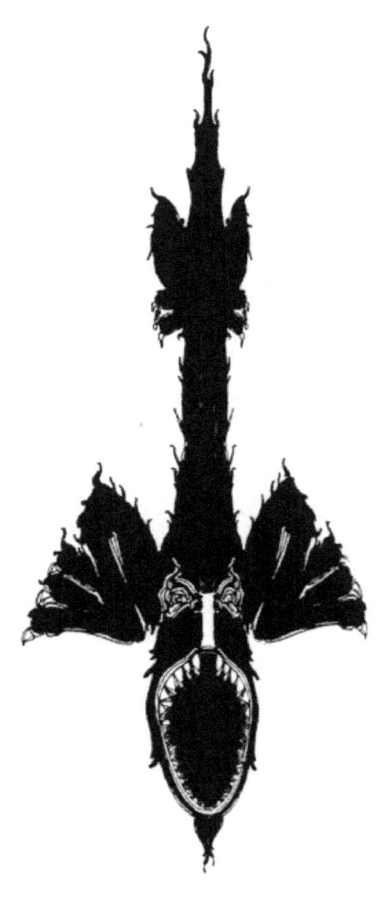

FROM THE PULP LIT PULPIT

New Year's Cheers

We begin our fourth year of publication at *Pulp Literature* with high spirits, bubbly wine, and significant changes. You'll notice slight format and style tweaks as we switch to a more bookshelf- and pocket-friendly size, but the biggest change is in the masthead. Founding editor Susan Pieters is taking a year off from the full-time editorial work to write her novels and short stories. While we're going to miss her invaluable contributions to the magazine, we celebrate her decision and eagerly look forward to reading the output of her pen.

Assistant editor Katherine Howard is stepping into Sue's shoes. Katherine has been a part-time copy editor and proofreader for the magazine over the past years, and we're delighted she has agreed to take on a larger role. Also joining our team are marketing and advertising coordinator

Rachel Kuo and bookkeeping 'mathemagician' Anat Rabkin.

We're thankful, however, that some things remain the same. We'd like to acknowledge the incredible work of our long time proofreader Mary Rykov and our copy editor Amanda Bidnall, who have been with the magazine since issues 3 and 4 respectively; our graphic designer Claire Milne who joined us with issue 5; and our poetry editor Daniel Cowper, who's been on board since day one. We could not put this beautiful magazine into your hands without them. The other thing that remains the same is our commitment to excellent storytelling across many genres and forms, from poetry, to short story, to comics and novel excerpts. In this issue, it's our privilege to present to you stories and poetry by extraordinarily talented writers. Sit back and enjoy them, preferably along with a glass or two of your preferred tipple.

Bottoms up!
Jen, Mel & Katherine

*I*N THIS ISSUE

Matthew Hughes brings masterful storytelling to two great tales as a twentieth-century statesman weighs the value of fate in 'The Devil You Don't' and a hapless investigator sees more than he imagines — and less than he should — in 'Fishface and the Leg'.

A hitchhiker and a band of aliens cut loose on a road trip from hell in **FJ Bergmann**'s 'How to Lose a Week', while an organ courier faces down a heart with designs of its own in **Rebecca Wurtz**'s prizewinning tale, 'Xuefei and His Heart'.

'Piano Music' by **Susan Pieters** uncovers a busy family's true heart; another family balances disappointment with beauty on a shoestring in **Jenna Park**'s coming-of-age tale 'Painted Nails'; and it's hard for kids to keep merry when there's a Santa-shaped monster behind the walls in **Anna Belkine**'s 'Better Watch Out'.

Anat Rabkin's beautifully drawn 'It Rained Then Too' tells the story of a relationship broken by agony and transformed by revelation.

A young woman faces dark magic and a cursed choice in **Carolyn Oliver**'s 'The Green Thread and the Blue', while a mermaid smuggler struggles with his career choices in **Eric Del Carlo**'s 'Mermail'.

In *The Case of the Cavalier's Rapier*, Book 3 of **Mel Anastasiou**'s Seven Swans Mysteries in Time, Spencer Stevens gets a second chance at happiness during the English Civil War; and finally, swordswoman Allaigna returns to our pages with gripping adventures rich in enchantment, political intrigue, and the secrets of a royal family in part one of the new serialized novel by **JM Landels**, *Allaigna's Song: Aria.*

THE DEVIL YOU DON'T

Matthew Hughes

Like the editors at Pulp Literature, *our feature author dips his toe in the waters of many genres, including biography and speech-writing.* **Matthew Hughes** *has been shortlisted for the Aurora, Nebula, Phillip K Dick, Endeavour, and AE Van Vogt awards for his fantasy and space opera, but he occasionally feels the urge to pull off an old-fashioned time-travel yarn. 'The Devil You Don't' combines that urge with the speechwriter's fancy of writing for one of history's most famous voices. It was first published in* Asimov's Science Fiction *in 2005.*

The Devil You Don't

The frantic sparks fly up into the November night like lost souls seeking safe harbour who, finding none, extinguish themselves against the unheeding darkness. Or so I might write it if ever I should put pen to paper to tell this tale. But I shall not.

The fire itself is confined by the blackened steel barrel. I poke again with the gardener's fork and another flurry of sparks shoots up, and with them scraps of burning paper. By the flickering light of the flames I can sometimes see a printed word or two before they are consumed: *Alamein, Rommel, Singapore, Yalta.*

The books are thick. They will take time to burn but I have learned patience. I have always taken the longer view. Perhaps it is a sense of history. Perhaps it is just how I am formed. But, in the arena of public life, he who takes the longer view must win out in the end.

The gardener has left in heaps his cullings from the bygone summer's flower beds. I gather another armful of dried stalks and withered blossoms and throw them onto the flames. The flare of light illuminates the disturbed earth that the gardener turned over this afternoon and the pile of red bricks that have lain here much longer—more than a year since I abandoned building a wall to take Mr Chamberlain's reluctant call.

First Lord of the Admiralty then. Prime Minister now. It is what I have always wanted, I will admit, though I would have preferred its arrival under less perilous circumstances.

The books are burning well. I leave them and kneel beside the wall. The cement with which to mix the mortar is just where I left it and there is water at hand. I lay a red fired brick atop the black soil, trowel its side with mortar, then place a second beside it.

Another pass with the trowel, then another brick. The work proceeds as it always did, a step at a time. That is how walls are built. As are lives. And futures.

The man appeared from thin air. I wanted to think he had stepped out of the darkness but the space behind him was well lit by the lights of Chartwell's great house, my house. I had not been here since the start of the war.

"Please don't be alarmed," he said.

"I am alarmed," I said. "My visitors usually make less startling entrances, and then only when invited."

"I mean you no harm."

"I am relieved to hear it."

"I've come from the future."

"Now I am alarmed anew," I said.

There was a policeman in the house, a Special Branch man with a pistol. But I did not call out. My visitor begged me to allow him to demonstrate his bona fides.

I did so and was soon convinced. He had a watch that displayed time through ingenious means and a device no larger than a calling card that could extract a square root in the blink of an eye. He showed me coins and paper money bearing the likeness of the young Princess Elizabeth, grown grandmotherly beneath the Crown of State.

"I am glad to know that the royal family endures," I said. "You bring me a heartening sign when one is sorely needed."

"I have brought you more than signs," he said. "I have brought you wonders."

He produced a package of books, small paperbound editions such as I had not seen before. I took them in my hands. The titles had a ring to them: *The Gathering Storm, Their Finest Hour, Blood, Sweat and Tears.*

Then I saw the name of the author. It was mine own.

"What are these?" I said.

"Your memoirs," he said. "The war years, at least."

"Then I survive," I said.

"More than that. You win."

"I am glad to hear it."

"It was touch and go for a while," he said. "But that was not the worst of it."

"Oh? Then what was the worst of it?"

I have not often seen a man look so forlorn. "The cost," he said. "The sheer waste. The horror."

I did not know how to comfort him. I set the books down on a heap of bricks then brought out cigars and offered him one. He seemed delighted to take it. His face shed its melancholy and he exhibited an exhilaration I have seen only in the shining eyes of schoolboys encountering their idols on the sidelines of a cricket pitch.

"I knew you would be here tonight, alone," he said, when he had puffed his cigar alight. He had studied my life, he said, choosing a night when I had come to the old place, away from memoranda and telephones and committees, to wrestle with my old black dog of a mood that had gripped me since the terrible raid on Coventry two nights ago.

He savoured the rich Cuban leaf, blew out a long stream of blue smoke, then said, "But now you can stop all of it before it happens — the Blitz, the Battle of the Atlantic." He looked wistful for a moment then continued. "My mother's younger brother drowned when his ship was torpedoed off Newfoundland in 1942. Fifty years later, she still cried for him."

"I am very sorry," I said.

"But you see, now he doesn't have to die," he said, gesturing to the books with the hand that held the cigar so that a scattering of ash fell upon the cover of the one entitled *The Hinge of Fate*. "It's all in there. Hitler's plans, his blunders. His invasion of Russia, D-Day, all of it."

I looked at the books atop the bricks but did not touch them.

"Now you can strike where he is weakest, shorten the war, save tens of millions of lives."

"Are there others like you?" I asked. "Other travellers through time?"

He told me that the channels by which he had come back to me were abstruse, unknown to any other. He had hit upon time travel by the most outrageous twist of odds. "But once I knew I could come here, I had to," he said. "The war was the most terrible thing that ever happened. But with these books you can prevent the worst of it."

"Hmmm," I said. "Show me."

He bent to retrieve one of the volumes. I reached for a brick.

I mortar a second layer of bricks over the first, tapping each carefully into line with its brothers. The man from the future lies with his wonders beneath the fire-hardened oblongs. His books are ashes now.

I wonder if he understood, as the light was going out of his eyes, that I must accept all the horrors to come. That is the price to be paid for the knowledge he had brought me, the knowledge that we will be able to endure and that then will come brighter days.

But would they still come if I had looked into those books? If I could see the present as the past through my own future eyes, would I not surely wander from the path that I now tread in darkness, though with a good hope that it will lead us eventually to those broad, sunny uplands?

I must choose the devil I know, though I know him now to be even more horrid than I feared, because the devil I don't know may well be even worse.

Yet the man from the future has not striven in vain. He has done much good. Because of him, my black dog is once more whipped back to his dark kennel.

I finish the second layer of bricks, stand and brush the dirt from the knees of my trousers. I lay the trowel on the unyielding surface.

I shall carry on. We shall see it through.

FISHFACE AND THE LEG

Matt Hughes

Matt Hughes *has won the Arthur Ellis Award for his suspense fiction. His mystery novels* Downshift *and* Old Growth *have been recently released as eBooks, audiobooks and paperbacks. You can find them on Amazon and on his website, matthewhughes.org. 'Fishface and the Leg', first printed in 1982, was his first published story and is based on real-life events.*

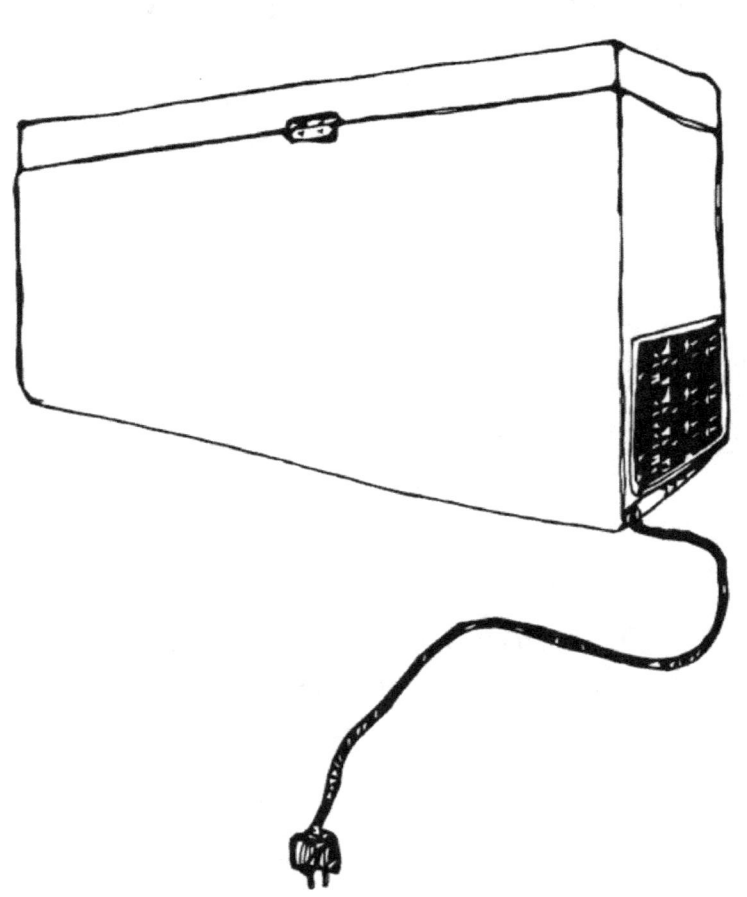

FISHFACE AND THE LEG

We always called him Fishface, though I'm damned if I know why. He used to put me more in mind of a fox—red complexion, sharp inquisitive nose, eyes a little too close together. But, within an hour of when he got off the train to be the new corporal at our one-man RCMP detachment, somebody had hung Fishface on him. I guess if you'd asked around town for the man's real name, you'd be lucky to find a dozen who could tell you.

At first, maybe we resented him a little because he took over from Corporal Matheson, after Bob went on to his just reward as a sergeant down in Regina. Everybody liked Bob Matheson, and nobody hereabouts really thought of him as the town cop. Sure, Bob was the guy who locked up Ernie Laderoute Friday nights, when Ernie had absorbed all the hooch he could wrap his hands around, but he also coached the kids' softball team through two district championships. Fishface, he was a whole different box of biscuits. He'd slope around town like a lost mutt, tall and stoop-shouldered, and you'd have to be a more charitable soul than the average to call him rangy instead of just skinny. The Mounties couldn't make a collar tight enough or a sleeve long enough to stop Fishface from shooting out of his uniform in all directions.

He would have qualified as pitiable if you hadn't always felt that he was just waiting for you to do something that would allow him to pounce. Fishface took a personal interest in the law. Throwing Ernie in the jug once a week wasn't meat enough for him; he itched for some real crime to test his mettle. But in the mid-1930s, there just weren't too many desperadoes lurking around Hubble, Saskatchewan, population 915 and dwindling.

I'm long retired now, but back then I ran the Hubble Funeral Home. Now, a lot of folks will tell me, "Stop right there; we don't want to hear about that," but I was not a bad mortician, and took pride in my work. I'd inherited the business from my father, and he had it from Grandad. I mention my line of work because it led to what happened to Fishface.

Pretty regular, I used to take the hearse over to the regional hospital — I won't mention the name of the town — and pick up bodies from the morgue. Often as not, I'd pass Fishface lurking in his official car behind some roadside blind, waiting to nab a speeder.

He might sit there for hours, and I suppose he occupied his mind with dreams of how someday John Dillinger or Alvin Creepy Karpis could come roaring by and he would catch them and be a hero. But, given the condition of the highway, and the placement of Hubble pretty far away from most bandits' preferred haunts, the best he ever got was some hapless commercial traveller or maybe a lost tourist. It'd only be a two-dollar ticket, but the recipients would get their money's worth, what with Fishface barrelling after them and practically running them into a ditch, siren shrieking and red light blazing, while his hopes and ambitions were inflamed.

Fishface had been among us a little more than three years when he thought he'd finally got his chance to be a major league crime fighter. It was late winter, and I had driven over to the hospital to pick up old Mrs Ellis, who had passed away. From my frequent visits, I'd gotten to know one of the interns pretty well, and we'd usually sit and have coffee before I made the run back to Hubble.

Well, this day, he told me he had a problem. "It's the incinerator," he said. "Damn thing's broke down — it'll be a week before we get the replacement part — and meanwhile, we've got this leg."

It seemed some poor woman had been flown down from up north with a bad case of frostbite, and they'd had to take her leg off to save her. With the incinerator out, they couldn't dispose of the leg, and they had no place to store it.

"You've got a cooler," the intern said. "How about you take the leg back with you and keep it until we get the incinerator fixed? You can bring it back next trip."

I guess I don't have to tell you I wasn't totally pleased with the arrangement. But a friend in need … We wrapped up the leg in some newspaper — it sounds gruesome, I know, but that's what we did — and I put it in the hearse with Mrs Ellis.

When I got back to Hubble, though, I had some second thoughts and decided I didn't want it lying in the cooler. So I put it in the trunk of my Studebaker. It was late February and well below zero day and night, so I thought it would keep just as well there as anywhere.

It was a couple of weeks before I had to go back down to the hospital again. I took the leg with me. I remember passing Fishface along the way, which gave me a little twinge. When I

got to the hospital, I looked for the intern, but a nurse told me
he was down with the flu.

I suppose I should have brought the leg out right then and
there, but there had been something decidedly informal about
the way we had handled the matter, and I was concerned it
might make trouble for my friend. So the leg returned with
me to Hubble, and went back into the Studebaker.

I thought about telephoning the young doctor and getting
things settled, but we were all on party lines then, and even if
none of your neighbours was listening, Mary Haggerty, the
operator, almost always kept her earphones plugged in. So it
was a good three weeks before business next called me to the
hospital. There was no body to pick up this time, so I went in
the Studebaker, with something in the trunk that I didn't intend
to bring back.

I asked for the intern.

"He's gone," they told me.

"What?"

"Gone to Saskatoon to work with the public health."

And he wasn't coming back.

Now, it seemed to me that there were only so many ways to
handle this situation. I could march into the hospital administrator's office and turn over the leg. I wasn't too sure what the
ramifications of that option might be, but I figured they wouldn't
reflect too creditably on my professionalism.

Or I could just slip the thing into somebody else's coffin,
hoping that the pallbearers wouldn't notice the extra weight.

Or I could dispose of it some other way.

One thing I could not do for much longer was to keep the
leg in the trunk of my Studebaker. It was already getting up

to April, with warm weather about to roll in. In the end, I did what many a young man has done when faced with a thorny dilemma: I went and bought a drink, and when that was of no immediate help, I bought several more.

By the time I was driving home along the empty back roads, the answer was no clearer, and I was not in too sharp a focus myself. But I recognized that the time of decision had come. About ten miles outside of Hubble, there was an old concrete bridge over the river. There the leg and I parted company. The ice was just breaking up, and the water was flowing fast with snow melt. The leg shot out of sight under the bridge, and I went home.

A couple of days later, some kids found it washed up a few miles downstream. Fishface was on the case.

Madge Schmidt, who did the typing and filing down at the detachment office, said it was just like Christmas and his birthday all rolled into one. He was down to the river taking photographs and measurements. He was on the phone to Regina and district headquarters. He brought in tracking dogs and hired an airplane, and the sub-inspector in charge of general investigations came to see him personally. It was Hubble's crime of the century—a murderer who dismembered his victim—and Fishface had come to glory.

He had every able-bodied man out searching for more pieces of the body. He formed us into squads, and we spent days slogging through muddy fields, poking into culverts and among the roots of trees. Fishface ordered schools closed and stopped cars all over in a one-man roving roadblock.

He was having the time of his life. But he wasn't having much luck finding a murderer or any more evidence.

After a couple of weeks, the fuss started to die down. The extra constables who had been seconded to Fishface's detachment were withdrawn. The newspapers went on to new sensations. No one on the missing persons list checked out as a likely victim, so the Mounties wrote it up as an unsolved case and went back to catching bank robbers and bootleggers, business as usual.

Fishface couldn't do that. He couldn't let it go. He tacked up this big aerial survey map on his office wall, all marked off in grids. The thing must have covered fifty square miles, and Fishface meant to search every square foot.

Week after week, Madge typed up his reports to headquarters, telling them where he'd looked and what he'd found. One time, he turned up an old axe out by the Kellerman farm, but it had been lying there a good ten years. And he did find Jerry Harnock's still and busted it up, which was a great disappointment to some.

But it got so that Fishface wasn't doing anything but look for clues to the leg murder. He even stopped throwing Ernie Laderoute in jail, and that brought a sharp complaint from Ernie's neighbours. Eventually, the RCMP pulled Fishface out of Hubble and transferred him somewhere else. Nobody shed a tear, and it turned out that the next corporal the Mounties sent us was pretty keen on softball.

But it's funny how one thing can pop up in a man's path and spin him off in another direction, for good or for ill. I think about that now when I see Fishface, trudging through some field on his old, arthritic legs, that big map rolled up under his arm.

It's not much of a retirement for him, living in a ramshackle, flat-tired trailer, spending his last days trying to solve a murder that never happened.

Sometimes I wonder if he lies awake at night, listening to the wind rustling through the grass, looking back on the mess that leg made of his life.

He wasn't completely wrong. Somebody did get killed. I wonder if Fishface ever realizes that it was him.

FEATURE INTERVIEW

Matthew Hughes

Pulp Literature: To borrow a phrase from your website, you've got a lot of hats you wear in the literary world right now: science fiction author, fantasy author, crime writer, and copy or developmental editor. Do you have a favourite hat? And are there any new hats you've considered trying on but haven't got around to yet?

Matthew Hughes: I've also recently written a historical novel that I had wanted to write for more than forty years. But fundamentally, I consider myself a crime writer trapped in a science fiction and fantasy author's career. Right now, I'm waiting for an agent's response on a suspense novel I've been working on for quite a while.

Most of my SFF stories have been about criminals and detectives. *A Wizard's Henchman*'s protagonist is an interstellar Sam Spade who discovers that the universe of space ships and thinking machines is about to be replaced by a realm of wizards and dragons.

PL: To the science fiction and fantasy world you're known as Matthew Hughes, and to the mystery and thriller crowd you're Matt Hughes. What made you choose different bylines for each genre? Have you found there are benefits or pitfalls to having two pen names?

MH: It keeps the different genres separate, which can be important when buyers for major retailers are looking at your numbers and deciding how many copies of your next title to order.

PL: *In* Downshift, *your first mystery novel, your protagonist Sid Rafferty provides us with a genuine — if slightly tongue-in-cheek — depiction of what freelance writing in Vancouver was like twenty-seven years ago. Do you think that the industry has changed between then and now? If so, for the worse or better?*

MH: I was a high-end speech-writer, working for CEOs of major companies headquartered in Vancouver. Like MacMillan Bloedel, BC Tel, Place Development, Viceroy Resources, Crown Zellerbach, BCRIC, and a number of others that no longer exist. If I was still in the business, I'd probably be relying on political clients instead of corporate, which is a much dicier field.

PL: *You've ghostwritten a couple of books:* Breaking Trail *(2000) and* What's All This Got To Do With The Price of 2x4s? *(2006). How was that experience and would you ever consider doing*

it again? Do you have any advice for anyone considering ghostwriting as an occupation?

MH: I might if the money was good enough. The advice is: get half the money in front and don't turn over the manuscript until you've received the second half. That wisdom comes not from the two that I did, but from another one where I put in a lot of work before I realized the client had no intention of paying me.

PL: *If any of your novels could be adapted for film or television, which one would you champion as the best work to adapt first? Conversely, are there any of your stories you're afraid of seeing interpreted on a production company's budget?*

MH: I've read and written enough screenplays to know that novels are generally too long for movies. They have to be simplified and cut down to size. Some of my short stories would adapt well. "Devil or Angel" (*Magazine of Fantasy & Science Fiction*, January 2013) started out as a movie treatment. And in 2004 I had a story in *Alfred Hitchcock's Mystery Magazine* called "Muscle" about society women who decide to hire themselves out as, well, muscle.

PL: Your newest book, A Wizard's Henchman, *makes a transition between hard SF and fantasy. Would you like to talk about your worldbuilding process and how you decided now was the time to finally reveal the collapse of the interstellar civilization called the Ten Thousand Worlds? We understand that you've crossed a temporal threshold with this new narrative that you haven't before now.*

MH: Many years ago, I came up with the notion that the universe might sometimes arbitrarily switch its operating principle from rational cause and effect to magic. I was thinking at the time of Sir Isaac Newton, the founder of the Enlightenment and the Royal Society, who started out as a serious practitioner of alchemy. I thought, "What if alchemy used to work? And then one day it didn't and he had to start all over from scratch?"

The conceit I've followed in the Archonate stories is that this switch is about to happen and the thousands-of-years-old technological civilization of the Ten Thousand Worlds will completely collapse. But only a few people know the end is coming. They're like the British diplomat in August 1914 who saw the First World War coming and said, "The lamps are going out all over Europe. We shall not see them lit again in our lifetime." And then the war came and Victorian-Edwardian civilization, with its grand and gaudy empires and its deep social divisions, fell apart and never rose again. Most of my characters have been like that diplomat, though some have been proto-wizards trying to hurry on the change so they can be in charge. In *A Wizard's Henchman*, I finally took some characters through the great change.

PL: *It appears that lately you have mainly been publishing your work through PS Publishing and Amazon. Does going through these publishers allow you more creative leeway than you have had with other publishers? I ask because your work is very experimental and unique, often bridging multiple genres, and that can sometimes be a hard sell to a large company. Do you believe that going through smaller publishers has allowed you more integrity as an author?*

MH: I've always written what I want to write the way I want to write it, and I've sold to big outfits like Time-Warner and Tor, as well as to smaller houses like Angry Robot and Nightshade Books. Lately, I've been concentrating on writing

for magazines like *Fantasy & Science Fiction* and *Lightspeed* while working on the historical and suspense novels. And I've been self-publishing my backlist novels and collections of my short stories that have run in pro markets on Amazon and my own web store. They're mostly good stories and they bring me new readers.

I'd like to see both the historical and the suspense books sell to larger houses, for the possibility of long-term returns (the historical would also make a great movie). I would really like to see the thriller — it's called *One More Kill* — get a good launch because the character is dear to my heart and I would like to write more about him. And as I said above, I am fundamentally a crime writer.

THE SEVEN SWANS: THE CASE OF THE CAVALIER'S RAPIER

Mel Anastasiou

How far will Spencer Stevens, then and now, go to find his long-lost love? Whether he's on horseback as one of the Cavalier soldiers of King Charles, spying behind Cromwell's lines; in the here and now and out of his depth with an iPhone, scouring the world for Holly; or struggling with a derelict pub in need of renovations beyond his strength and skill, Spencer is an unlikely hero, but one who'll stop at nothing to take a second chance at finding happiness.

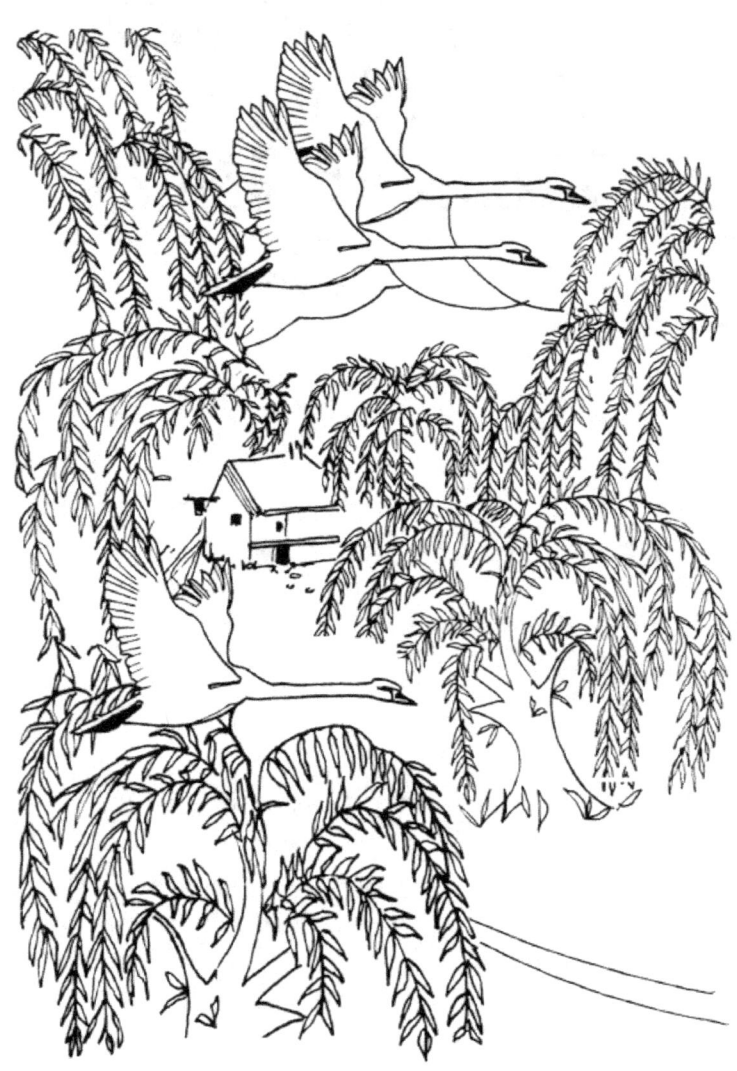

THE SEVEN SWANS, BOOK 3: THE CASE OF THE CAVALIER'S RAPIER

CHAPTER ONE

The bartender at the Old Bearded Lamb, a mile up the canal from the Seven Swans, leaned over and slammed a fizzy water down in front of me. It was my third, and fizzy water is served without charge in most pubs. It had hardly gone eleven o'clock of a sunny June morning, and the only other customers in the place were a couple of Guinness-breakfast-of-champions old fellows. I had the distinct feeling that if Byron, my dear friend and lifelong enemy, had not been ordering the latest in a parade of pricey fruited Pimm's cups, the bartender would have taken me by one ear and frogmarched me out the pub door.

"Sorry," I muttered. "I can't take the booze."

"So? Why does my business have to suffer?" The publican looked from Byron to me. "Why don't you take something else on the menu, then — nachos grande, or a pukka pie?"

"Most barmen are more sympathetic with the customers," Byron said. "That's just a little hint to help build your business. We'll have crisps, then, and none of your smoked salmon or chili-flavoured rubbish crisps either."

I said, "Salt and vinegar, please."

"One pack." Byron put his hand on his wallet pocket. I hoped that meant he was paying.

"Two packs," snapped the barman. "For a start."

Byron waved a hand. "Do your worst."

The barman turned away.

"What an unlikeable fellow he is." I peered into the shadowed corners of the room.

"A marketing moment, if I've ever seen one." Byron called out to the old boys, "Hoy!"

They looked up from the bottom of their Guinness flagons.

"How's the Guinness here, anyway?"

"It's crap," the nearer fellow said. Both in the spry zone of their eighties, the one who'd spoken was wide and strongly built. The other was thin, his shoulders rounded protectively about his pint.

The thin one said, "I timed the barman, didn't I? The pour, I mean. Thirty seconds or I'm a Dutchman."

"Too fast by half … No, by …" Byron frowned. "By four and a half minutes, anyhow. It ought to be a five-minute pour, or I'm from Hertfordshire."

"You, from Herts?" The old fellows cackled and sucked at their Guinness.

"You see?" Byron said to me. "A thirty-second pour, and yet this bar has custom. If that cranky, fast-pouring bastard of a barman can do it, then so can you."

"Your logic is flawed," I answered.

"Unlikely. How so?"

Conscious that the Guinness drinkers were following our conversation, I answered softly, "Because, I would be a publican who doesn't drink, can't cook, and worst of all," I added, "who doesn't care. A man has to care about his job or he'll be rubbish."

"True." Byron had been a banker, a ski pro, and a tennis court salesman, and was rubbish at all of them. "But you're trapped, aren't you, by your ex-in-laws and your great love for your long-lost Holly, exactly like Dante. And like him, you've got to give it the old college try."

"Here are those crisps," the bartender said, setting two crackly bags on the counter in front of us. "Cheese and onion's all we've got."

Byron handed him his debit card. "I was telling my friend here that he should take your course in customer relations, to help him run the pub he's reopening."

The barman looked me up and down. "You? The teetotaller? What pub are you opening?"

I sipped my fizzy water and gestured in the general direction of the canal.

Byron said, "The Seven Swans."

The man looked from Byron to me and then at the door. He roared with laughter and threw a third packet of crisps onto the bar. "On the house," he said, and walked off.

I ripped the first bag of crisps along the seam and laid it open on the bar between Byron and me. We had shared many things besides crisps, he and I, including my wife, Angelica, now his lover. Ten years before, it had been the other way round. But I had sworn off trying to get Angelica back again, because Byron really loved her, with her long legs and terrifying parents. The same parents who had gifted me, a dry alcoholic, with the Seven Swans Pub.

"What am I going to do, Byron?" I asked. "Seriously, the

Seven Swans is a blackened shell, the roof is Swiss cheese, and nothing works."

"The toilet works," Byron said. "I had a whizz, and the flush was both timely and symmetrical."

"But seriously, there aren't any electrics—"

"Surely you're wrong. The place wasn't closed until '87."

"No electricals that work. And if the Old Bearded Lamb here, with its painted walls and cold fizzy water, isn't getting custom ..."

"It's got ours," Byron pointed out. "And these two fellows with the Guinness. Where's that phone I gave you?"

I pulled out his iPhone. "It never rings."

"That's because nobody wants to talk to you. Remember, I gave you this phone so that you could hunt down your youthful sweetheart from forty years ago and bring her back into your arms where she belongs, incidentally abandoning the field of combat for Angelica's heart, which you neither truly want nor deserve."

The two Guinness drinkers were gazing at us with obvious enjoyment.

"Well, that was only the beginning. This iPhone"—Byron held it up like a tennis racquet ready for an overhand lob—"is also for contacting contractors."

"Contacting contractors," the thin Guinness drinker chortled. "Say that twelve times quickly, will you?"

"I will, if it becomes necessary to do so."

I smothered a laugh. "I don't know any contractors."

"You do now, because Angelica's father has seeded this phone with numbers of his cronies and his cronies' friends who specialize in plastering, plumbing, and refrigeration."

One of the Guinness drinkers asked, "You going to hire some London people to do serious renovations, then?"

"Yes."

"To come up from London to work on the Seven Swans? Like, drive up the motorway to the canal?"

"Yes. It's an hour's drive."

"On the M25?" The two old fellows chuckled into their pints.

Byron and I stared down at the phone. "Don't forget that Angelica's parents are allowing you two thousand pounds a month to fix up the Seven Swans."

"So you say," I said. "I haven't seen a single pound yet."

"You will. And you'll have to live on it while you're renovating. And pay your credit card charges. The dear old School of Life fees."

"You know what I could do?" I asked. I pulled out my wallet and opened it to Holly's picture. She smiled up at me, twenty when it was taken, although now she would be sixty, just like me. She was somewhere out there. "I could let the credit card charges rot, take the phone and the thousand pounds a month, and fly to America." I would start on the East Coast and work my way across the continent looking for Holly. It wouldn't be much money to live on, but if I took a nylon tent, like when we were young, and a sleeping bag and bought food at grocery stores, it would have to be a better life than this one.

I sipped my soda water in the Old Bearded Lamb and imagined myself a sixty-year-old Jack Kerouac, riding the roads of America, ordering apple pie and ice cream out of silver-sided diners. Byron drank his Pimm's and shook his head between sips.

"Your ex-in-laws have set up automatic payments for the banks. Two thousand a month."

I came back to earth. "I hope they realize I'm not going to renovate the Seven Swans any time soon on that."

"Not only do they realize it, I believe that is their cunning plan."

They meant to keep me out in the country and away from their daughter Angelica, my former wife. "Bloody high-handed of Papa and Maman."

"Not really, since they're paying you. But this *is* high-handed: they have actually roped in a spy who will be reporting your progress on the Seven Swans. If you leave, the money stops. Then the spy lets the banks find you and start cutting off your toes or something."

I narrowed my eyes at him. "You're the spy, aren't you?"

"Yes."

"Damn." I shoved the phone back into my pocket.

"Cheer up. You can still look for your old girlfriend Holly. You'll just have to do it while you're painting and spackling."

A future packed with grout stretched out before me, grey, fathomless, and grimly DIY. I held out my hand. "Where's my thousand for this month?"

"It's on your credit card, for renovating costs. And on a Waitrose card for food. Angelica's family has shares in John Lewis."

"The nearest Waitrose is at St Albans," the Guinness fellow said. "An hour on foot, if you hop it."

"Two hours if you hop it on one leg," the other chuckled.

I scowled. It helped me think. "Byron, not only are you going to report back to my ex-in-laws on my progress, you're going to pick up supplies in your car. And you're going to lend a hand with the hard physical work."

"It would be nice to think so," Byron said doubtfully.

"And one more thing." I was sick and tired of losing to Byron

Standard-Clarke. I would get something out of this, or bust. But what?

"What's that, my longtime friend and rival?"

"My friend here is buying more Guinness for these two fellows here."

As it turned out, the old fellows, Stan (the strong one) and Eustace (the narrow one) were the only two who left the Old Bearded Lamb happy that day. They were full of Guinness, and they clapped us on the back and wished us joy in grouting and plumbing as they saw us out onto the street. There, they lit cigarettes and disappeared magically into the smoke. Byron and I found ourselves alone at the soggy corner of the village green, with nowhere to go but home.

"Home, home, tra la," Byron said gloomily.

I kicked at a low crumbling wall and dislodged a brick into the roadway. "All right for you. I have to go back to a long day on the canal bank, and then curl up to sleep like a dog in a summer-weight sleeping bag in a smoky brick cavern. You're going home to a new townhouse and a warm bed."

"Ha. I am going home to Angelica, and it is week one of cohabitation. We both know what that means."

I did know. "It means gluing down shelf liners under her direction until 2:00 am."

"And receiving noisy bollockings on the subject of constructing additional shelving."

"And enduring personal remarks about fading muscle tone while pushing enormous sofas and dining tables of oak and granite from one end of the place to the other."

"And then back again, because she didn't like it after all."

"Yes."

We both sighed. Me, because I'd lost Angelica, and Byron no doubt because he had her.

Chapter Two

The following morning I sat unwashed with my back against the canal, drinking warm orange squash out of a family-sized bottle. I watched the narrow boats go by, and such were the wide-eyed stares of the voyagers hanging off the stern that I finger combed my hair and buttoned up my shirt. I decided not to shave. Angelica called the first three days unshaven my Italian Film Director look, which gave me one more day until my shaky descent into the condition she called the French Film Director look. Then I walked inside, through, and around the Seven Swans pub, spinning about suddenly to catch the angle of a glassless window or the curve of the battered plywood bar, thinking that it really wasn't so bad after all. Thinking it again. And not believing it at all. I tell myself stories, but this one was not so much embroidery of the fancy as it was a big-ass lie.

"What am I supposed to do with you?" I asked the pub.

For answer I received the usual rusty smoke odour up my nose.

Aloud I continued, "How am I supposed to make you into a pub? I've been living in London for forty years. You can't even hammer a nail into a wall there. I got a man in to put up our Christmas tree. I hired a woman in to unplug the guest toilet. I ..."

I stopped. The place was laughing at me, a low old man's chortle appropriate to the age of the place. I could hear it quite clearly—as clearly as I'd lately seen the girl with the arrow stuck in her back in the fourteenth century, and the red-headed Tudor princess taken unawares by an assassin. The laughter echoed around the room, out the side bar, back through the kitchen and pantry areas, and up through the holes in the roof to the clear blue Hertfordshire sky. No doubt up there the angels were laughing at me, too.

The laughter died after a moment, replaced by a hacking, gurgling cough and the sound of somebody spitting on stone behind me. I turned and saw Stan and Eustace, the fellows from the Old Bearded Lamb the day before. Stan, sturdy and pleasantly red-faced, had his fists deep in his pockets so that the rounds of them stood out firmly at about the level of his balls. Eustace, skinny and pale, was mushing something about on the threshold stone with the toe of a battered loafer.

Stan was saying, "No, you silly bugger. You don't use spit on the threshold, there's no luck in that."

"Maybe. But better that than slitting the fellow's throat as they used to do and sprinkling blood about to keep the devil out of the new building."

"Who did that?" I stepped out of the smoky shadows into the clear morning air. "Nobody used to do that, did they?"

"'Course not. This is Hertfordshire, a garden county," Stan said. "We're just taking the mickey."

"Extracting the urine, as it were," Eustace explained. "And a little spit for luck can't hurt, can it?"

"That's true as Sky News," Stan said. "Can we come in and have a butcher's, then?"

"That's a 'look'," Eustace explained. "In Cockney slang. To rhyme with *butcher's hook*, you see."

After four decades in London with this Canadian accent of mine, I had had more Cockney rhyming slang explained to me than Covent Garden tube station has "apples and pears," and furthermore these two elderly Hertfordshire lads were no more Cockney than I was. But I realized with a lifting of my spirits that I was glad—no, grateful—to see them. I begged them to come inside the Seven Swans. Once inside the bar room, Stan tutted and Eustace shook his head.

I told them, "I don't know where to start renovating the place."

"Ah," Stan said. "I can see that the walls will have to be taken down to the brick, the brick will need to be repointed all round, and that's a rare old job. Number two filler, would you say Eustace?"

"I would."

"And mayhap a good scraping and refit about the windows ..."

I was staring from one to the other. In the few moments that had passed since they stepped inside the pub, they had transformed from two old Guinness lovers in ill-fitting trousers to angels of mercy and genius.

"Stan. Eustace. Do you know how to renovate a pub?"

"I don't. But I've seen it done," Eustace nodded firmly.

"Done by you, Stan?"

"Right you are. Construction, bricklaying, plasterwork, and whatall."

"Man and boy," Eustace said.

"Well, I'm sure you'll knock this job on the head. Good luck." Stan led Eustace away.

They ambled off along the canal path in the direction of the Old Bearded Lamb.

I ran after them. When they turned, I waved my arms humbly

at the hopeless structure on the side of the canal. "Will you fix up the Seven Swans, then?"

Stan stared at the pub and sucked his upper lip. "The work won't come cheap, whoever takes it on."

"Oh no no," Eustace agreed.

"I've seen it before in the building trade," Stan added. "Sometimes a fellow like you gets an idea, and that idea is better than the real thing. You might just want to let it be. This place is a dog's breakfast, my son."

A funny thing happened to me when Stan said the Seven Swans was a dog's breakfast. When he said those words, something inside me I thought long gone, smothered by years of Angelica and her pretty ways, revived. That something was rebellion. For I looked around the pub, from grubby walls to blackened ceilings, from rubble-strewn floor to piss-poor plywood bar, and I was irritated with Stan for calling the Seven Swans any kind of disgusting meal, including one meant for a not-too-particular dog.

I wanted to say, "It's not that bad." But it was.

Or, "The Seven Swans has got great bones." But the best bones had been bricked into the rear of the fireplace in Tudor times.

So I played the drinks card. "When this old place is put right, I'll serve Guinness. And give it a five-minute pour. Right?"

Stan and Eustace weren't listening. They'd gone out and round the back and I could hear Stan say, "Can you credit these old electricals?"

"Early workings, then?" Eustace asked. "Aside from those eighties wires?"

"Oh yes, Antiques Roadshow won't have seen the like. Our fizzy-water publican here is sitting on a gold mine."

"Oh, yers, yers."

I heard a couple of light thumps against the outer wall and knew that the pair of them had fallen against it, laughing. "Bloody old bastards," I muttered.

They must not have heard me, because next moment Stan and Eustace were back in my midst. "The place is not so bad," Eustace said.

"No, no," Stan said with the air of a physician who did not believe in giving a patient bad news. "Not so awful as all that."

"Good," I said. "Where would you start?"

Stan and Eustace took a long moment to answer. They looked left, they looked right. They gazed out the door and up at the hole in the ceiling. At last Stan asked, "Do you have a million pounds at all, my old son?"

"No," I answered. "Just the thousand a month Byron mentioned at the pub last night."

"Ah. Well, then, I suggest you roll up your sleeves and give the place a good old clear out. Or you can chuck the whole thing for the day, come with us, and pour a good black Guinness down you."

I shook my head. "I'm fizzy water only. No booze permitted. Still, how can you do it, anyway, you fellows: drink Guinness at nine in the morning?"

"Keeps your bowels open as daisies," Eustace said.

Stan nodded. "Yes indeed. My old dad lived to a hundred."

"On Guinness for breakfast?"

"No, he never touched the stuff."

"But if he had—" Eustace grinned. His teeth were good.

"Yes, if he had, he might have lived to two hundred."

I wondered what the Seven Swans would look like if more roses grew around the place. If I put up a bollard nearby at the side of the canal, would any narrow boat stop? What if a whole family climbed out to order lemonade and crisps and lager, which I supposed that I could serve them out of a picnic hamper?

Or an ice chest.

The idea filled me with an unexpected sense of power. I felt like the younger son in a fairy tale, the Fool who is granted magic and insight beyond his ken. The character who might or might not rise to be worthy of such a fine transformation.

What if I did as Stan suggested and only fixed up the exterior of the place? I could paint the bits of surviving plaster on the outside walls and artfully leave the ancient brickwork showing. Have a sign made, and put out picnic tables, strewing hanging baskets from every branch and beam. Whitewash the toilet, which flushed. The idea took hold of my brain like a pressure headache, one of those fist-tightening ones that paracetamol with codeine can't touch.

And then?

I pictured myself handing out crisps and packets of sandwiches with the supermarket label torn off, cress and egg, prawn and salad cream. Cracking a lager for Dad. "No, sorry, youngsters, you can't go inside the pub, I'm afraid it's under renovation. Have another crisp, won't you?"

It would be a pretty way to pass the summer. In between narrow boats, I could search for Holly on Byron's smart phone. So long as nobody asked for my license to sell crisps and cold canned Carling, I could probably clear ...

... a good ten pounds a day. Hmm. I could just about eat on

that if I ate my own sandwiches, and buy myself a pair of socks or something once a year. Still, it was ten pounds more than I was making now. It was with a tingling feeling that some great change was coming for me, and my credit card to hand, that I heard a familiar voice call out. I went round to the canal side and there stood Byron, with a canned steak and kidney pie in one hand and a six-pack of fizzy water in the other.

A brick flew out of the Seven Swans doorway and landed with a crack on a concrete paver. Byron started, and we both took a step backward. Byron tottered dangerously on the edge of the canal bank. I caught him by the yellow cashmere sleeve of his cardigan and pulled him back solidly onto his feet.

Byron shuddered. "I might have died."

I patted his shoulder. "You mean you might have swum."

"Spence, do you know what's in canals?"

"Effluvium."

"If 'effluvium' is another word for toilet waste."

"If it's not, it ought to be. Look, you're fine, and anyway the boats have to empty their tanks into ..." — I was out of my depth here — "a tank emptier thing ... tanks for emptying tanks. You know."

A dozen more bricks flew out the pub door.

We approached the door together. "Eustace? Stan? What are you fellows doing in there?"

Eustace answered, "There's a problem."

More bricks flew out. I said, "I don't think I can afford new bricks."

At that, Stan stepped out through the door. He was smoking a pipe, with which he gestured at the jumble of brick at our feet.

"You don't want to rid yourself of these bricks, old son. They're gold. Worth a king's hoard. You'll want to use these to fill in any holes in the wall."

"Really? How big a king's hoard are they worth?"

Byron shook his head. "Put that thought back in its box, Spencer. You can't sell the pub for cash, not even the bricks. It's in the papers Angelica's parents wrote up."

"Anyway, you don't want to sell this dear old girl." Eustace jerked his head towards the pub. "Even though she may be unsound."

"Unsound?"

"That's right, break that news to them gently," Stan said, leading the way inside.

"Do you mean it's dangerous?" I asked, following Stan, with Byron and Eustace at my heels. "I sleep in here."

I blinked in the semi-gloom.

Byron approached the bar and leaned over it. "What traps and obstacles dwell in this black pit of a kitchen?"

"Bit of a nightmare, true. Follow me and Eustace just round here, but watch where you step, my lad. Here, I'll put on the lamp."

He turned the light on and the glare blinded me. "Sorry, lad."

"Turn out that bloody light—"

Stan said, "Watch your step."

Eustace said, "Mind your language."

I walked into a hole in the floor. One leg went straight down the hole, and the other stayed up on the ground. It was an extremely uncomfortable position. Stan and Eustace, making noises that cover snickers, bent down and took me under the armpits and attempted to lift me out. The brickwork round the edge of the hole was very unsteady.

"It's an old kitchen well," Stan said. "Very desirable in the olden days. Dip down into the well and get your water, easy as pie."

"Or fall in as easy as pie," I said testily, one leg still stuck in the well. "You'd better not be thinking this is funny, Byron."

Byron, watching from the other side of the bar, said, "I was just thinking, better you than me."

"Why is that?" I asked through my teeth while Stan and Eustace pulled.

"I've got longer legs. Who knows what's down there?"

"Spencer, you're a weighty old thing," Eustace grunted.

"He's still got his boyish figure," Byron said.

For answer Stan and Eustace dropped me. My leg fell a little deeper down the well, and my foot touched something down in the hole. Something hard.

"Byron, help me out of this, will you?"

"For heaven's sake." Byron came round the bar and the three of them took hold of me and pulled hard. I came up a little way, and then the brickwork gave way and the four of us tumbled down. My leg descended even further, and a sudden agony sliced through my trousers and up along my calf.

I did try not to make a fuss while they were pulling me out to lie on the filthy floor of the bar area, my injured leg throbbing, my back aching, and me doing my very best to swear in a sustainably quiet manner.

"Get him outside, will you?" Stan said. "I'll see whether I can find out what it is ... give me that bit of iron bar, no, the long one. I'll try to fish it out."

Byron and Eustace helped me to my feet and got me round the bar and out the door. I tried not to look at my leg. "Some bricks fell on me recently," I said, "And now this. Do you think the pub is trying to kill me?"

They shook their heads and gazed at my ripped and bloody trouser leg. Eustace held back the edge of the rip and the two leaned in closer.

Byron said, "This looks pretty bad. We'd better bind it up."

"We'll use my shirt." Eustace unbuttoned his collar, but he got no further than that, for Stan was exiting the Seven Swans doorway, the length of rebar in one hand and, in the other, an ancient, very rusty sword.

"This old weapon is the culprit," Stan said.

"Fancy old Cavalier thing, isn't it?" Byron said. "From my fencing days, I can tell you it's a rapier."

"Pretty pointy as swords go," Eustace said. "What do you think about a doctor for Spencer, lads?"

"It may come to that." Stan put his hands on his hips. "Spencer, I think we'd better let you bleed a bit. Out with the bad. Hope your tetanus is up to date."

"Tetanus? Lockjaw, wasn't it, in olden times." Byron poked gently at my trouser leg. "Now Spencer, we're not still swearing, are we?"

"Yes, we are. But, I've had my tetanus. I'm fine." I felt dizzy, and the pub seemed to loom up around me. I wanted nothing more than to get away from it, and from them. "Just, give me that thing."

Stan passed me the sword. It was all rust, except for some bits of black leather stuck on with little studs, and much heavier than I would have thought. I stood up and waved back Eustace, Stan, and Byron a step or two with it.

"I'm going to look at this in the sun. By myself."

"Are you sure?" Byron frowned. "That's a sword wound, my friend."

"I'm sure. I'm a rock. A whingeing, bleeding rock of all-rightness."

"Let him go," Stan advised. "This sort of thing happens all the time on a building site; you don't want to encourage complaint."

Byron snorted. "*Swords* happen all the time on a building site?"

"Who's going to carry him if he keels over?" Eustace wanted to know.

I left them bickering and wandered off, sword in hand, around to the north of the Seven Swans, across the sunlit bit of grass that ran beside the canal. Illogically, fervently, I wanted nothing more than to get out of the pub building's sight. I ducked under a fringe of willow branches into the green-lit natural tent beneath the tree. Hidden from the world, I sat on the good earth among the willow's twisted roots, holding my trouser leg tightly around the place on my leg.

I stared down at the graceful, rusty sword lying across my lap. My vision blurred and dimmed.

CHAPTER THREE

At Oxford, amid the shuffle and chaos of a war going wrong, the King himself insists that I have my portrait painted for my twenty-fourth birthday. The blue and red oils Van Dyck used before he died have run low, and slurs of brown paint and clever use of negative space draw on the surviving portraitist Mr Dobson's talent, which is luckily a deep well. The picture requires a nearly unending series of sittings, and I mean to endure them all. Not because I intend to send my portrait back to Hertfordshire to my long-lost Corianna, nor out of pride, which on all of us Cavaliers is thinning faster than the soles of our best boots, courtesy of Essex, Cromwell, and the rest of the

Parliamentarians. No, I sit for that portrait to please my mother. She desires my likeness because all she has of my two younger brothers now are bits of lace from the brims of their hats. She wears the lace looped around her wrists so that she may touch them when she wakes and before she sleeps. I would rather give her a hat trim than what is turning out to be an overly flattering painting of myself, but I fidget through sittings between battles, for she reminds me that I am the last of my line.

The other ladies sharing the chilly don's room envy her me, for so many of them have lost all their sons. But before Mr Dobson can dot the shine on my nose with lead white, my father dies of fever from a pike wound in his thigh. I take the next sitting as seriously as my mother did, but now while the artist and I debate the angle of my hat—straight to show loyalty, or angled to indicate bravery when outnumbered in battle—my mother sinks like a wounded swan among the grubby silks and velvets pooled about her lady friends. Now there is nobody but Corianna who will care what I look like in oils. It seems to me that she would hardly care more for a painted memory than she professed to feel for the man himself during our final argument before I left for war. So I thank the King's artist, and as soon as he leaves I put my knee through the half-finished canvas—which one should never do; it smears a brown stain on my best remaining blue silks—and mount my horse for battle.

I mount my father's best horse Noble and ride with my comrades out of Oxford, our swords bouncing, our horses' hooves clattering over the cobbles. We pass the old students' residences, jammed these many months with blueblood mothers, aunts, and sweethearts, grubby and weeping. I see that I am riding only three rows back from the King, an honour due more to mortal wounds others take than any prowess with my sword. (As a child, I shirked fencing lessons for running through fields and woods with my peers.) How proud my parents and younger brothers would have been to see me so close to the front line. It is cold comfort, like a belly full of yesterday's porridge, but the thought carries me for ten miles. When the King rises on golden heels in his stirrups and raises one dove-grey glove in recognition of his forces, his gesture raises my spirits for another ten.

At dusk, I draw aside into the willows with two other fellows I know, and we relieve ourselves into a trickling brook, asserting that the King will carry all; that Rupert knows what he is about; that training, brains, and God will get us through Cromwell at the end of the day. Both of my companions have wives at home, large with second babies. They lace up briskly and jostle each other out of the willow shadows. They are older than I by at least two years, and ten years older than my brothers were. I tie my laces slowly. I follow my companions back into our lines, and when darkness falls, while men light fires and pitch shelters among the white-flowered hawthorn, I slip away into the trees and water and feed Noble, wondering all the while whether I am a fool or a dead man. Both seem likely. After a long time staring at the stars with my arm over Noble's warm neck, I reach an answer. So I turn my back on my fellows. I salute the King. I ride Noble into the shadows and gallop him southwards, towards Hertfordshire, where Cromwell and his troops are gathered. Since the enemy holds Hertfordshire, Noble and I steer clear of important roads.

Nighttime in the countryside is black as coal, for the King, with all his divine rights, has not seen fit to provide us with a moon. But I know the roads. Even better, my good horse was foaled in my family's barns, and he rocks me towards home. By the small hours I'm sound asleep in the saddle and dreaming of my duty to my family and King. By the time I wake it is well past dawn on this fresh April Wednesday morning. Wednesday is market day, and I believe I smell cattle on their way for purchase. Noble has carried me within a few miles of St Albans Abbey and my family home near Kingsbury Mill. Somebody else holds it now, a Parliamentarian of note, my mother learnt. That evil will need to be remedied some day.

Just now, home is not my aim.

The sky sweeps rainclouds overhead. I shelter among trees at the riverside near the Redbourn crossroads. Here I finish with mud the job Mr Dobson's paint began on my blue silk trousers. My padded jacket lining is grey with the sweat of four years' war, so that is all right. I cut off the tops of my high boots and toss them into the narrow river, brown like the mud and the tiny sturgeon I used to catch here as a boy with my bare hands, the best among my friends at patient waiting, if not at fighting. I take my knife and a last bit of bread and cheese from my leather wallet, chewing on the latter while I hack off my curls with the former, as close to my head as I can manage while leaving both my ears where they belong. Wallet and hat I toss into a low thicket. I wrap my sword and scabbard in a ragged bit of brown cloth that had long ago been red and draped a Roman-style chair that my grandfather had commissioned for a visit from Good Queen Bess. I tie the sword to the saddle. The rain lets up and I lead Noble along little-used paths I know well, until we reach the flatlands below the Abbey. All of us, the market-goers, cattle, and geese, keep to Holywell Hill, away from the soldiers gathered in the flatlands where the cleared area near the old Bell public house is dotted with the cold morning remains of Cromwell's soldiers' campfires. As I cross, keeping to the wooded lanes, I peer at them. They look exactly like the Royalist campfires. I would bet my scabbard that these men, like my own comrades at ease, are talking proudly of their wives, round with child, back home.

I know the area better than these soldiers can, having in boyhood run and shouted through the tunnels of rowans and willows by the River Ver. Noble and I creep through the undergrowth to a spot near the riverbank and camp, somewhat pillowed by dew-damp ivy through the daylight hours. I lie on my back and gaze up through the rattling branches at the crows, dead black against the blue sky. Finally I sleep, and Noble wakes me too early with a tug at the toe of my boot and returns to foraging in the long grass with his flat teeth. I set my back against a rowan tree, picking lover's petals off tiny spring daisies, and counting the boyhood friends I'd played with in these shadowy hiding grounds. I add to the list my young brothers, whom we used to scold and chase away with long whippy twigs. All dead. Except me, and Corianna. I shut my eyes again, wishing for nightfall. I get my wish as one of the enemy's fires crackles and sparks to life. A man not far off swears and laughs. I rise from the warm earth, hating soldiers. Hating us all.

CHAPTER FOUR

April in Hertfordshire is the season of white flowers, especially the tiny daisies that brighten the daytime greenery and encourage us to name every day summer. As dusk approaches, pale blossoms are an aid to children's chase and hiding games, because to seekers our faces are not the only white bits in a leafy world. I apply this principle to myself, grown now, and a King's soldier, knowing all the time I should be ashamed of keeping hidden like some poacher or thief. Now, as the darkness grows deeper, so does my conviction that riding boldly into battle in my bright blue silks would have been be undutiful to my cause. For I am one of the King's army of soldiers, and I am the last of my family's name.

I am glad that I kept my family's sword. If I turn up to claim her without it, what would my sweetheart Corianna think? Or her cantankerous father, Mr Randolph?

"Well, Noble, dear old steed, what do you think? What will Corianna say to me?" For I've had reports that my letters reached her safely, until the Roundheads took all. And she's never answered any of them.

"Will she be at her home on Catherine Street? Will she lean out her window and call out to me, *Spencer, how lovely. See, your ring is back on this chain around my neck.*"

I tuck the sword more carefully under the saddle and tie its ragged wrapping with a few of my torn blankets over it. It will be my death if it is found. More than that, it will be my dead father's second death, and my grandfather's, all my scions back through to the War of the Roses, where my Lancaster ancestor was sole survivor of our family as well, for although he died he left a boy baby, born into the English peace that connected him to me. We came over with the Norman King William, and so did Corianna's family, although hers married into the Raleighs and lost their fortune in Sir Walter's rough fall. If Corianna still loves me, she will marry me. If she lives, she will certainly marry me, though she swore through her tears to me the night before I rode to war that she would never speak to me again in this life or the next.

But some things a man knows, and although she said she hated me, and may say it still, I know that once she calms down she will remember that she loves me and none other. I had better be certain, because to desert my King, hide my sword, and crawl through the bushes like a rabbit is a serious sacrifice to make for the woman who scratched my face and told me I was the devil for leading my hotspur fifteen-year-old brothers into war.

I decide not to creep. I can't ride through town even at night and expect to live to marry and sire a son, but I can lead a horse through the fields like any stable hand. As I guide Noble out of the undergrowth, I am careful to keep equal distances between me and this night's campfires to right and left. As the closest fire flares up, I spy an armoured soldier, helmet doffed to show his swarthy face, rise to his feet and turn his gaze towards me. He lifts a mug, which I would bet is filled with beer from the nearby Bell public house. I thank him for the lesson in how not to look like a Cavalier. For even in his armour his shoulders are rounded and his chin pushed out in front like a shovel. I hunch my shoulders, with apologies to my dead mother, and shove my chin out as well. I tug at Noble's bridle to make him drop his neck. Ahead I see the old Bell, and amid this mess of enemy soldiers, I try to be an everyman. So I walk where any man would walk — towards the old public house as a point on the path to St Catherine's Street and Corianna.

I lead Noble among the thick-strewn tents and greasy fires of Cromwell's army. With every step I take I apologize to my revered ancestors for my slouching steps. Silently I remind them that I have a woman to wed and a child to sire, for my revered ancestors as much as for myself. After all, if they hadn't taken the time from their wars to wed and procreate, my family line would have disappeared before Henry VIII straddled the throne.

I sidestep a slippery bit of offal in the grass near a bubbling, delightful-smelling cooking pot. A fellow in the sweaty padded underclothes that Cromwell's men wear beneath their armour sets a tin of beer down on the trampled earth beside him. He frowns up at me.

Tugging Noble's head lower, I step between my horse and the soldier. If I speak a word he'll know me for an enemy. My words, learnt at my gentle mother's knee, will give me away as easily as if I were to sling my broad-brimmed feathered hat onto my head and trumpet, "God save King Charles." So I lower my head and pull at Noble's reins to move us past Cromwell's soldier and his cooking fire.

But the soldier barks, "You, there. Whose horse is that?"

I do not look towards him, for I am a soldier and doubt I can master the challenge in my gaze. I walk on. Noble's hooves make a crunching sound upon the rough rocks hidden in the grass. Round about me the skinny shapes of swords and pikes stand near to hand and famously serviceable. The soldier gets to his feet.

He says, "You're walking about General Cromwell's camp, among his best men. I advise you to answer me, for you'll be one of his own yourself, when you come of age."

This is galling, for I came of age three years before. I swallow my protest, suck on my upper lip, and slouch us away from him. However, there's no disguising a truly fine horse, and the lift of Noble's hoof and the angle of his ears give away his eponymous background. At the same time the soldier leaves his beer and moves towards us. Round about, others of Cromwell's army look up from their discussions, their fires, and the mugs of beer in their fists to stare at Noble, me, and Cromwell's soldier.

There's no avoiding it: I stop. I resist lifting my chin to quell the fellow with a glance. I decide that one-word answers, grunted as the men who worked my father's land grunted them, are my best chance to leave these fires to their owners and continue on my way, unskewered by pike or sword.

"Whose is the horse, damn you?"

I answer, "Dunno."

"Don't you? Let me see. I know a bit about horses." He moves closer.

I move away, tugging Noble with me, nearing the old Bell. If something doesn't change soon, the situation will call for me to show my mettle as a fighter.

I move more quickly, not quite trotting, and as the Bell looms up before me, I can see inside the downstairs casements the bar room, lit by candle lantern. There's a warm glow of safety within, and promise of food and drink. A group of serious men, soldiers all, are gathered around a table, studying something on it. Maps, I guess. Up above it another window shines yellow and promises a good bed, for the old Bell is famous among its neighbours for being almost free of bedbugs and spiders. As I gaze upwards, a slender woman in a white mob cap moves into the light at the window. I so long to see Corianna that I think it is she, and that she is looking down at me almost as if she were looking at me, although even with the soldiers' cooking fires spotting the field around the pub the night is too dark for her to be able to make out an individual man's face. Of course I know that this girl is not she, for Corianna is an aristocrat and does not sleep in pubs. Nor would she wear a married woman's mobcap, for she will marry me and no one else.

The soldier who knows horseflesh is hard on my heels. "Whose mount is it, raggedy?"

I choose two words, and fasten them together with a slur. "M'master's."

"Listen, the scarecrow speaks," a nearby soldier says ironically. "It wags its tongue and words hang in the night around us."

"Like stars in the strike-me-down sky," another soldier adds.

The first soldier sniffs and scowls from Noble's soft black eye to me. "Where are you taking the beast?"

The other soldiers are on their feet now, some with a bit of bread or cooked chicken or pork in their hands. "Yes, where?" "Where's its master?" "I think the lad is absconding with the horse."

"Absconding? Through the middle of the lot of you soldiers?" I burst out, and there follows a silence.

"Say that again, will you?" the first soldier says.

I answer, "Wot?"

Another soldier demands, "Where are you taking the horse?"

"Yes, who's he for?"

I look again at the soldiers on the other side of the window inside the pub. I am inspired with a single word that ought to end their questions and cause them to let me pass. "Gener'l."

"What did he say?"

"What did you say?"

I answer, with as much awe and respect as I can manage to put into the cursed name, "Cromwell."

Chapter Five

When the soldiers hear the general's name — Cromwell, famously efficient, and hot-tempered as the devil himself—they take a step backwards. It seems that my lucky stab may lead to our escape, for if I act my stable lad part with clever stupidity, perhaps they will rate me less a danger than their fearsome general and move off farther still. They might even leave me and my war horse entirely free to pretend to search out Cromwell, so that I may carry on with my search for my intended wife, Corianna.

The soldiers, a dozen strong now, glance at one another, at me, and towards the Bell. I pet Noble's flank, admiring the stars overhead, the little stack of chamber pots outside the pub door that somebody had been cleaning—probably that pretty girl in the mob cap at the window up above the room where the senior officers nod their heads *yes* and *no* over their plans. I am a stable lad, though, so it does not do to look at these when there is a girl in the window above. I am faithful to Corianna, but must look my part, so I fasten my mooning gaze upon the girl in the upstairs window. She places her hand on one of the small leaded panes and pushes it open—which one should never do, but open it by the wooden part—and looks out, her white cap and fair hair shining in the darkness. The soft light from behind her illuminates her lovely face before she moves away back inside the room, out of sight.

I let go of Noble's rein, slack-jawed as the lout I'm pretending to be. I just manage to stop myself crying out Corianna's name. For it is she—I am certain it is she—at the window of the public house.

The soldiers continue debating, and I am half-aware of the malicious looks they cast from me to my steed. Noble stands with his usual untroubled aristocratic poise. I scowl up at the window, while my mind seethes with certainty and foams with doubt. It can't be Corianna. The thing is impossible. Gently raised, and full of strong opinions, my affianced would no more step foot in the public house than ride naked down the street like Godiva.

The soldiers move closer together in the discussion. Only warm yellow light flickers inside the open window.

Corianna. I haven't laid eyes upon her in years. Perhaps this mob-capped girl only has the look of her: fair and slender, eyes set wide apart. For I must admit that every woman in the world has the same number of features, and mathematically speaking there are just a few differences among them—complexion fair or dark, eyes set wide or narrow, nose short or long. Anybody, with a brief few seconds to take in an apparition, might make an error.

But what kind of a man doesn't know his own sweetheart? Or remember the star-bright night when she said she might marry me, if only I didn't take myself and my brothers to war? Even dressed as a servant girl she is my Corianna, my wife to be, and the future mother of my heir. And, out of the thrill of realization, a terrible question arises. What is she doing in the pub where Cromwell and his officers sleep?

Perhaps, like me, she is a Royalist spy, here to learn Cromwell's plans. She is clever—cleverer than I, as she often used to make me admit. She has the intelligence to remember any schemes and numbers she might overhear, and to repeat them without error into an official Royalist ear. But she doesn't have the temperament—just a temper. Corianna can no more stand among a crowd of Parliamentary officers and soldiers without denouncing them than General Cromwell can resist giving battle wherever he goes.

And with that I know the answer. My Corianna has been taken captive. The Parliamentary Army are holding her in the pub, away from the common soldiers, for even Cromwell's men must see she's no common prisoner. They must be looking to ransom her, or to exchange her for an officer. I hear reports that we Royalists have several enemy officers as well under lock and key, every man of them panting to return to battle. Parliament have more of ours, of course, and what a cunning plan it is, to trade a gentlewoman for a lieutenant, while they keep our own warriors gaoled and out of play.

The first soldier raises his arms widely. "Cromwell's got one horse in the pub. They say it's worth a fortune."

"Like this." Another nods at Noble.

"I'll take him in," says a third. "I outrank you fellows, so to me goes the glory of the moment."

Catastrophe. All is lost.

Without thinking I grunt out, *"General Cromwell said."*

These are magic words, for with curses and buffets the soldiers wave me on towards the pub. What if I were to nod a mute thanks to the soldiers, make a pretence of approaching the pub door, and carry on past into the darkness beyond, in the direction of Corianna's family's house on St Catherine's Street, and so gain news of how she had been captured, and help with her ransom somehow? But it will not do, and I squash all thought of my own escape as unworthy of a Cavalier. I have no hat, no gloves, yet I am still a gentleman. I straighten my bearing.

I stand tall. As if he senses my mistake, my horse Noble gives me a terrific nudge with his head. I turn and meet his soft dark gaze. It seems to say, *Better a Cavalier and his lady alive to carry on his family name, than striding sword held high among the legions of aristocratic dead.*

Life is a mystery. The mystery, of course, is how to go about staying alive. So I slouch again, the better to rescue my Corianna, and vow silently to get us out, free, and away from Cromwell's army and his own formidable person. I hold Noble's reins and take a step towards the public house. Another. Inside, along with Corianna, my affianced, I will find Cromwell and his lieutenants. Or else they will find me.

When I was a big-eyed, tiny child in skirts, my old nurse, as nurses do, told me tales that dripped with blood and terror. The idea was to keep me in my cot at night, yet as the real tale of my life emerged her stories also prepared me for the red days of hard warfare. For example, only a week ago a bare revolutionary blade took off my poor cousin Henry's arm at the elbow. Since Henry's death, when I shut my eyes I see the spray of his blood as it hit my white shirt, like angry words one can't take back, and continued for a longer time than you might imagine. And I remember just as clearly the arched portal in my nurse's story of Handsome Lord Wolf, who took to himself a new wife each evening and devoured her, fingers to toes, overnight. He set the latest pretty head on his windowsill next to the previous, so that the dawn would strike bright lights from her long maiden's hair. To my leery eye, Handsome Lord Wolf's portal looks exactly like the door of this public house. And Cromwell, except for his average looks, is to my mind not much less dangerous than Handsome Lord Wolf.

Wolf or no wolf, in war, a soldier moves towards danger, not away from it. So I take another step towards the portal—I mean to say, the pub door. I plan to tie Noble's reins to a trellis near the door. Not that he needs it, for Noble is too well born to move until required to do so. I decide on the spot, for I have after four years a soldier's way of thinking, that the next move is to enter, bypass Cromwell and his men, and take the stairs to the first floor.

I peer at the candlelit interior of the bar proper. So bright is it that Cromwell must have requisitioned every candle in the shire. Therefore, I can't insinuate myself through shadowy corners and doorways to pass Cromwell and his men.

If I am to pass without comment, I will need a reason to do so.

What would a roughly dressed fellow like me be doing in officer's quarters? Not cleaning, for that is what Corianna in her married woman's mob cap must be pretending to do. I scan the yard outside the door in the light from the bar for a chunk of wood. If I find one I will carry it inside and upstairs, as if I were a servant who had been commanded to keep the fires of the Bell pub burning. Once out of sight of the Roundheads I will be free to search the upstairs rooms for Corianna. I will spirit her back downstairs, just two busy servants exiting the public house. Then we two shall leap on Noble's back, Corianna snug in my arms, and gallop away with a Cavalier's chance at a clean escape.

But there is no lump of wood anywhere to be seen on the cobbles around the pub door. None under the eaves to right or left.

I turn my back on Noble to search under the bar window. Nothing. I scowl, racking my brain for something different that I might carry upstairs. So furiously am I thinking that I start at a sound I know well, the aristocratic whicker of a battle horse. It isn't Noble, for I know his whicker and anyway he would never betray me in the dark, among the enemy. The sound comes from nearby, and indeed when I peer through the window into the main room of the pub I see its source clearly. A fine chestnut horse is tied up to the bar.

Nobody has to tell me it is Cromwell's mount. One should never tie a horse to a worthy publican's bar, for it is discourteous in the extreme, and the General is famous for his lack of manners. In fact we in King Charles's army reckon Cromwell as gifted with less honour than a weasel in a butcher's shop. As I peer through the window from outside, that aristocratic steed tied to the bar is a sight so uncouth that it reduces the General's power to terrify. As well, now that I see the horse, I know how to get inside without being arrested, interrogated, and head-spiked before dawn like one of the Handsome Lord Wolf's young wives. I turn to Noble.

I murmur, "We're going inside, Noble, my friend, and I make you three promises. First, that no Englishman, not even the devil Cromwell, will harm a wellborn horse like you. Second, that no matter what happens, I will come back and free you, even if I have to do it as a dead man risen in the form of a ghost. And, third, that you will overhear a lot of blunt language from Corianna when I take her away from her spying, but don't worry, for although she'll mean every word, I feel certain that she loves me still."

I step ahead of Noble and he ducks his head to clop through the tallish pub door directly into the bar. Never has a public house room seemed more brightly lit in all but its furthest corners, nor the night at my back seemed darker or more attractively equipped with hiding places and escape routes. I look once over my shoulder, catch Noble's liquid, confident gaze, and turn to face the King's enemies.

Cromwell's lieutenants are still crowded about a large map lying open across one of the public house's several tables. As they raise their heads to look at me, it is like the several petals of a buttercup opening to the dawn, if only they'd had long, shining locks like my brothers and me, and not short-shorn heads like the Parliamentarians wore to fit more easily into their helmets. I remember gratefully that I too hacked back my hair.

Cromwell leans back against the bar, a small beer at his elbow, stroking the nose of his pretty steed tied up there beside him. Noble's hooves sound like gunshot on the flintstone floor.

I grunt, "Horse." I drop the single word but I recall with a start that I am still a soldier, and the rules of combat applied.

I must now call Cromwell by his rank and name because whether he knows it or not, he is engaging with the enemy. Me. The scion of my house. I try again. "Here is a good horse, General Cromwell."

One of the lieutenants stands up. "Where'd you get him, then?"

I answered, "Better not to ask."

"Then I won't ask you his name. I'll give him one myself. What a creature you bring me, fellow." Cromwell shifts his weight from the bar to his boots. His eye is alight with the gleam of an avid horseman. He approaches Noble, and without another glance at me, snatches the reins out of my hands. "Come here, Swiftfoot."

Swiftfoot. Well, like his master, Noble is able to bear anything for duty. I stand aside, eyeing the officers gathering round Noble to congratulate the General on his taste in horses. To my right a steep bricked stairway climbs towards the second floor. It is by no means in shadow, and any man climbing it, or descending with a furious young woman in tow, will be hard pressed to hide his comings and goings. Still, first things first, and getting my Cavalier backside upstairs will make a good start. The trick will be not to look suspicious or wary. This is easy for me, raised by my mother to keep my shoulders low and relaxed, and never to move too slowly or too quickly, nor to glance at persons of inconsequence, not even out of the corners of my eyes. I mount the steps, at once relaxed and intent on searching for my Corianna, while below I hear Noble's whinny, and that of the first horse, followed by the uneven clatter of horseshoes on the flint stone floor no doubt being tied up to the bar. I confess that before I attain the top step I feel cold to my toes, for although I thought

I might just manage to impel Corianna, disguised as a chambermaid, down the steps and safely out the front door, I have no idea how I would extricate Noble from Cromwell at the bar.

And strapped to his saddle. My sword. A Cavalier family weapon of honour. Sooner rather than later, with a fine horse like Noble, they will groom him properly. And that means removing his saddle and everything tied to it. So I had better be swift. And Corianna? She had better be silent.

I move up to the top of the stair, seeing nobody, yet feeling a certain sense that I am being observed. The landing is empty. I take a deep breath and open the first of three doors into the upstairs chambers. One swift glance inside the first room shows me a bed large enough for four, unoccupied. The second room's floor is scattered with bent breastplates, bashed-in helmets, and trestles that look as though horses might have trampled them — not Cavalier horses, however, which are much too sensible.

I shut that door and open the third. Corianna stands between the stripped bed and the open window, a bundle of linens under one arm. A thick vine of purple wisteria bisects the window, and she is holding tight to it, as if to hold herself upright.

I say her name. I approach her.

She pushes me away, but I imagine I see relief in her expression. "Then you're not a ghost?"

"Certainly not." How can she think such a thing?

"It would be just like you to come and haunt me," she says fiercely. "Now, go back where you came from, before we're caught together."

She throws her armful of bed linens onto the floor. She bunches her skirts in her hands the way she did when we ran or climbed together as children, and swings herself out the window, onto the wisteria vine.

Just as when we were children, I follow her. I sling one leg over the windowsill. Noble is down below, and I promised not to leave him. Still, I must stop Corianna first, for she is my own true love, and the mother of my family's family.

I am halfway down when Corianna sets one small foot on the ground among the barrels outside the pub wall. Even when we were children together—hating one another and laughing together and throwing mud at each other down by the stream-bed—I could always read Corianna like the family Bible. Now as I climb from the vine down onto the ground outside the pub I watch her turn her head on her swan-like neck to look at her avenue of escape through the trees, which would take her away from me, and from the soldiers by their fires, with their cooking pots, mugs of small beer, and eyes for a pretty pub girl. Corianna thinks she might run away from me. I know better, so I am not worried, or not very worried, especially because, since childhood, I can outrun her.

She looks up at me and scowls.

Starlight lights her face, and the wind rustles the leaves on the trees all around. I consider that not a bad last sight and sound in a man's life.

It's just like Corianna not to want to be rescued. And just like her to look at me like that. She returns the few steps in the shadows of the pub walls.

"Spencer, how could you survive the war so far and still be such a fool as to turn up here, of all places in the known world?"

I perceive that this is a rhetorical question. No one can understand the vagaries of war, of why some live and some die. I say,

"Corianna, what are you doing wearing that married woman's mob cap?"

"Oh, blast. Trust you to ask the wrong questions. I can't be seen with you."

"Aha," I hiss. "You're a spy. Like me."

"A spy? I'm ..."

"What?"

"I'm going to rescue you." She takes my arm. "We're going to walk slowly away through those trees just there. If anyone stops us, you're my weak-brained brother-in-law, who came to gaze on Cromwell so he could tell his grandchildren about it."

"Leave our grandchildren out of it," I tell her. "For now. Your plan is not too bad, for a woman who has not been to war, but honour won't permit us to follow it. I promised my good horse Noble, whom I know you remember with affection, that I would rescue him, and any design for saving you—"

"—for saving *you*—"

"—must include him."

"I'll return for him tomorrow morning early," she says. "I'll come back to set table for breakfast and steal him away then, while everybody is at their oatcakes and honey."

"Corianna, a soldier knows that even the most intelligent of horses cannot understand abandonment. I sleep in the stables at Oxford, and he hasn't been without my company for more than a few hours since the war turned against us."

She peers at me in the moonlight. "Are you saying that you plan to walk in and take your prize horse out from under Cromwell's bony nose?"

"I am."

"How?"

I scowl. "I will have to enter, reveal my true loyalties, challenge Cromwell to single combat, hope to get my sword out of its wrappings with all celerity, and have at him. I think I could win."

"Oh, Spencer."

"No, really, I'm younger than he is. Then I will spring upon Noble, gallop him through the doorway and out here again, swinging you before me on the saddle, and away."

"That's your plan?"

I nod sharply.

Corianna says, "In order to save your neck, I think I'll go and fetch Noble now and be on my way."

"The place is jammed with enemy soldiers, Corianna."

"They won't hurt me."

Before I can stop her, Corianna turns on her heel and marches into the bar. I move a little to my left to see what she is saying to Cromwell and his men in the bar, and whether any muskets are aimed her way. But she is gesticulating and men are gazing at her with offensively attentive eyes. Now they all turn towards the window, and all at once I see that she is pointing at me. I stand still, for if the blow were to fall, and that on account of my own true love's betrayal, I will meet it straight on, the way my father did in '41.

But the window clears of Roundheads, and the door opens. Out steps Corianna. She raises a hand in farewell to those inside and returns to me holding Noble's reins. I see in the light from the window that my sword wrappings are still strapped to his side. I feel slightly breathless as I take Noble's reins from her and stroke his nose, and I wish I had my hat.

"Thank you, Corianna. How did you manage it?"

"Perhaps I challenged Cromwell to a duel, and won. I'm even younger than you are."

"I hope that our children will have your sense of humour," I tell her.

"Oh, Spencer. Very well then, I told the General and his officers that you, a stable lad, had come to say that Noble had escaped into a field of fresh green and would soon be filling the air with the gaseous and liquid conversion of said grass, and is thus the last horse in England they should tie up to the bar."

I frown at her. Noble doesn't deserve that sort of calumny. But I thank her.

"Now, Spencer, walk like a stable lad."

"Not with you." A second later I'm in Noble's saddle. I swing Corianna up into the saddle before me, and we gallop off into the trees.

Chapter Six

We don't gallop for long, because the trunks of rowan trees are thick about us and the sky overhead through the rustling branches is nearly black, so it's impossible to see clearly farther than a few yards ahead. My horse Noble knows better than I how to pick his way through and around the trees. I relax my grip on the rein and tighten my arm around Corianna's slender waist. She gives me a sharp look. I loosen my grip slightly and after a moment she leans back against me. Her mob cap brushes the tip of my nose, and I sneeze.

She doesn't bless me. I cast about for something to say to her

"I have taken leave of the army without ... leave. Just to see you."

"How brave."

"Thank you."

"How brave to miss all the battles, just to see an old friend."

If I have ever worried that I was not yet grown into a man who can manage life with a wife, I prove in this moment that it is not so. I keep quiet. Noble walks and trots on though the rowan woods, and after a moment Corianna looks back at me with an unreadable expression. I tighten my arm around her waist a little more, and this time she lets me.

I knew it. But there is still the question of the mob cap and her descent down a wisteria vine. "What were you doing in that pub? You are a nobleman's daughter, and that is a commoner's pub."

"I am a commoner now," Corianna says.

"That's not for you to decide," I remind her.

"I run a pub. The Seven Swans, down in Hemel. And I do extra work in the Bell, now that the soldiers are here."

We are headed that way now. George Devon's pub, down by the river Gade. "War is a terrible thing, Corianna. Did the Parliamentarians steal your father's money?"

"But you must have known: my father never had money, only pride and our house. The army has our house, and my father's still the proudest man in Hertfordshire. But he's a proud Parliamentarian."

"Good Lord." Mr Randolph, a third son of that revered family, a Parliamentarian.

"And I can't run a pub and be Royalist anymore."

"You can if you come with me, and marry me in Oxford." *Or escape to the Continent.* This new thought surprises me.

"I can't."

"When we are married, you must not run pubs anymore."

"Spencer, don't say these things."

"Not for me," I hasten to say, "but for our children."

There follows a pause, during which I try to guess her response to such a leap forward in our relationship.

She says, "Here's a question that I challenge you to answer honestly. Can't you see that things are different now?"

I counter with, "Here's one for you. Tell me, why are you wearing that married woman's mob cap?"

"Why do you think, Spencer?"

In the silence that follows her question, I hear a thrashing noise behind us, like the noise Noble makes as he canters through the branches. Only multiplied. I say, "That is the sound of at least ten horses."

"But why should they be following us? They should not."

"They are." I kick at Noble, and he speeds up.

Corianna says, "Give me the reins."

We're not children anymore. I am a soldier, and Noble is my horse.

She adds, "I know the way to my own pub better than you."

She takes the reins and nudges Noble with her heels. He leans into a gallop. I hang on to Corianna's waist, as I used to do when we were children galloping across fields, among the cows, and all we had to fear was falling off into the big wet pats. Now we gallop among trees with swinging branches that threaten to knock us to the forest floor as the riders behind us draw nearer. High hopes would reach for Cavaliers at our tail. But this is Cromwell's town now, so high hopes would be stupid ones.

We leap a narrow section of the River Ver. Will the hoof beats follow? If they leap the water as well, we are lost, for ten horses will catch one in the end, even Noble.

They do not cross behind us. Eventually, Corianna pulls back on the reins, and Noble slows.

She says, "My husband ran the Seven Swans." I remember the Seven Swans and its burly master, George Devon.

I blurt out, "You are wedded? And, to a publican?"

"That is a very poor question, Spencer."

I try again. "Your father let you marry a publican?"

"My father had little say in the matter, but he had announced for the Parliamentary side by then and had no real objection to me marrying George, who was a good publican and a very handsome soldier."

"A Parliamentarian, then?" Corianna, married to the enemy.

"George was a good man who believed the King was a bad man. So he went to war for Parliament, and on one of his leaves, he married me."

"I'm sorry, but I must ask: what kind of a man lets his wife work in a pub?"

"A man who likes to see his wife each day, perhaps."

"Interesting," I say politely. Corianna is married.

She huffs out a breath. "A man who is dead, Spencer. Devon was among the five thousand killed at Kineton."

"I'm sorry." I take a breath. Corianna is widowed. "My brothers, too."

Silence. And now, a furious whisper. "I told you not to take them. I said how it would be."

I chew on the acid in her words as Noble gallops. Above us the treetops are shadows threatening at any moment to strike rain down upon us. A wind blows up and rattles the leaves around us so loudly that I can scarcely hear the riders at our backs. But I do hear them. And then I hear the crash of thunder on the left. I think about asking Corianna to speed our pace, or kicking at Noble's side myself. I know my horse's abilities, and in the darkness, he is already outpacing himself. And Corianna? Her mob cap hangs a little to one side. She leans further over Noble's neck. We make a sharp turn, narrowly avoiding a low branch that slaps at my cheek.

All at once we are out of the woods, tearing down a slope to the hundred-year-old pub by the river. Although it seems nobody pursues us, we approach the river at a gallop, and for a moment I believe Corianna plans to make Noble leap the span of water and take us out of reach. He might do it, or it might be the death of him. And us. I determine to stop her and as we clatter onto the cobbles outside the pub doorway, I reach for Noble's reins. Corianna hauls back on them, and Noble stops outside the pub door. I see what she means to do and leap off my horse's back to offer her my hand and knee to aid in her descent. She leaps down, her linen skirts making an arc in the darkness. Above us I see the crooked roof of the public house, and the chimneys, none of them emitting smoke. The place does not look wealthy. I think of George Devon, married to Corianna, gone for a soldier, and fallen in the same battle as that of my brothers, and my father. I think of King Charles, sweeping through Oxford with a smile and cascading feathers and lace, keeping up the spirits of his loyalists. I try to see one side better than the other, and meanwhile Corianna ties Noble up outside the Seven Swans. I follow her inside.

I don't know what I am expecting, apart from the usual smells of stale ale and ashes. One candle only burns above the bar. And in the light of it I make out the shadowed but unmistakable figure of Mr Randolph, Corianna's father, leaning against the bar. He is elderly, but so fierce that as always I forget his age, until I see that he is leaning on his elbows. And from his hands dangle a pair of flintlock pistols.

I stop, sword at the ready, but not lifted in challenge. Corianna runs round the bar to her father. This is not the time to ask one of the leading aristocrats of the area why he is standing behind the bar of a labourer's public house in shirtsleeves with his beard grizzling round his mouth and his hair clubbed back so skew-whiff that he might have done it himself. Instead I hasten to say, "Mr Randolph, I apologize for the intimacy of the ride, but you can put your pistols away. I had no idea that your daughter, affianced to me since we were sixteen, had married another."

"Shall I shoot at him?" Mr Randolph asks his daughter. "If I miss, will honour be satisfied?"

I say, "Yes."

"No," Corianna says firmly. "You must keep quiet, father, for the sake of our old life before the troubles came, and when the soldiers come you must say that Spencer is your nephew, and a good Parliamentarian."

Mr Randolph gives me a cold look. "Look at the mud on the fellow. He's too filthy to be my nephew."

"Devon's nephew, then, come to help out after an injury incurred in war. Father, you must do as I say."

"It will be the first time," he grumbles. He keeps hold of his pistols.

A rattle and slide of hooves outside the door and we all turn. Corianna runs to the window and raises her hand to those outside. Nobody has to tell me these are soldiers. I know without looking at them, by their comradely shouts and guffaws, for only soldiers act so unafraid in wartime, whatever we may truly feel.

Corianna says, "Open the door, father." She snatches my sword from me, and runs with it into the kitchen. There's a clatter as she bangs it against something hard, but almost at once the noise is covered by the sound of a dozen soldiers entering the public house. They are plainly dressed, and well shorn. Cromwell's men.

Mr Randolph's scowl lightens slightly as the men call for drink. He pours a glass for everybody, including a very dirty, very quiet nephew, that is to say, me. We all quaff together, with a cheer for Cromwell, except from me. The soldiers say that there's a sheriff in St Albans who's dared to stand up for the King. They're going to show him to the people tonight, on his way to jail.

"No stoning, of course," the captain says. "General Cromwell is very firm. Vegetable matter only to be thrown."

"Perhaps somebody will find some large tough carrots," one of his men adds.

The captain said, "I only wish that there were more Royalists to parade. For the General's sake. Don't you, Mr Randolph?"

Put on the spot in this way, and being of an old family, I can hardly blame Mr Randolph as he tells them that I am not his nephew after all. He explains exactly who I am and that I stand for King Charles. Of course Mr Randolph has little reason to defend me, but I must say that it is a disappointment to me, and perhaps to Corianna who emerges from the kitchen, without my sword, in time to see a soldier take hold of each of my arms and march me towards the door. She follows us and mounts Noble, clearly intending to ride him all the way back to St Albans. I'm glad that she has him. I know that Corianna, even with what are clearly not-unmixed Parliamentary views, will care for him when I'm gaoled. Or dead. I'm hauled up on horseback like a woman, in front of the captain.

The captain's breath, fresh with beer, tickles my cheek. "We are off to see a big-bellied official proclaim for the King up Holywell Hill, by the Abbey. I think General Cromwell will be very pleased if you will stand at his side to represent the King."

The soldiers riding closely enough to hear his words laugh. I'm not certain why until I see Corianna glance with pity from my shorn head to my torn and stained shirt of finest linen.

"Looking at this one, nobody will have to ask how the war is going," another soldier adds.

"They'll tweak his nose in gaol," says a third.

"Tweak his neck, more likely. So that he won't go and kill anybody else's brave sons."

"Ay, and yours were bravest, Richard."

I wonder whether Corianna will tell them of my brother's deaths, brave as this soldier Richard's boys, but she says nothing, only stares ahead in a thoughtful way as she rides. She's a lot more careful with her tongue around Cromwell's men than with me, and I wonder whether this is another sign of how the war is going. I picture myself, a soldier in gaol, doing the King's cause no more good than a rusted sword.

Soon enough we're back at Holywell, where once a saint was beheaded and flowers bloomed where his blood spotted the ground. Or a wellspring arose, or something miraculous of the kind. I can't remember now, for there's a crowd gathered on the hill outside the inn by the cathedral. Market day is over, but there are cows and swine being driven out along the road, and carts full of complaining chickens and geese clattering down the cobbled hill. The air is thick with smoking oil from their torches and lanterns, and they're in a noisy, rumbling rage that doesn't bode well for the sheriff, or for me.

I look around me at the soldiers, despising them for their treatment of me and simply for being the enemy; but then I remember Richard and his lost sons and think that one of these men could have been Corianna's George Devon. I feel ashamed, and in an effort to be civil, all soldiers together in war, I say to the soldier beckoning me to dismount, "I was just in St Albans not much more than an hour ago. There's a lot of riding hither and thither in war, isn't there?"

"Move your high-born arse off that horse." The soldier helps me down, again as if I were a woman, while Corianna leaps nimbly down from Noble. I wonder how best and most memorably to say farewell to her, for surely she will someday marry again and tell her future children about this night. Overhead the clouds are as dark as the oily smoke down here, and shadows leap under the horse's hooves, Noble among them.

The horses move Corianna and me, stumbling, together, and I say, "Farewell, Corianna. I wish you much joy in years to —"

"Quiet," says Corianna. "I'm going to start something. Wait until I say the word, and then run."

"What word?"

"Pigs."

It's true, there's a run of pigs moving among us, shouldering man and beast.

"Come with me."

"I won't leave —"

"Your father?"

She shakes her head. "I was a married woman, Spencer. Use your wooden head. You must know what that means."

"What?"

She cries out, "*Pigs!* On the loose." Quick as fire, she kicks the two nearest horses hard in the poor devils' shanks, steps in front of me, and backs me up into the noisy crowd to the timbered wall of the inn. She says loudly, "Hurry to tell the General that we need more of his men in the crowd. Pigs!" And shoves me off down the hill. I hear her call out after me, her words of farewell. "Faster, you fool! Tell the General." I run faster, away from the crowd and away from the one woman in the world who might have given me an heir. Or might have given me any happiness at all, except the joy of dying for a worthy cause. But what is that, in the end? For if the King's cause is worthy, then didn't Corianna's husband die for nothing? The world grows more unfair with every step I take away from Corianna and Noble.

It is dark, but not full dark, because of the clouds gathering in a mob overhead as I take hidden lanes and overgrown pathways leading to the hill that will take me out of town. I know every step up this hill: here, the great fern marking the end of a spreading line of horse chestnut trees; there, the three stones we called the Grey Man's Stairs. We always ran up this bit, my brothers and Corianna squealing with mock fear at my heels, and I with a stick for a sword, raised for their protection. Today, I trudge past the Grey Man's Stairs, wishing for Noble, longing for Corianna. Rain begins to fall. I am glad of it, not so much for myself—although cooling, sensible, discouraging rain will deter a full-blooded pursuit—as because it's bound to scatter the crowd rumbling about the poor sheriff in his silks and laces. It won't save him from gaol, but it might from a mob and a gibbet.

The rain pounds through the leaves of oaks and rowans and splashes on my head and shoulders, running down the length of my back and halfway down one thigh. As so often, I muse that the cooling, sensible rain is the reason for England's temperament in her peaceful years. I know there have been some. I've read my history. The truth is that it's agonizing times like these, in strife and slog, that make for good reading. I imagine a book about this war, printed and bound in the future. Reading it is a thin fellow with a pulled-back forehead and thick stockings bent over a book about the Cavaliers. I wonder whether we will matter so much in the end, with our superb horses, gloves, and hats, as he gazes back at us.

CHAPTER SEVEN

I struggle onwards, up the familiar way out of town, not moving as quickly as I would like, straining to hear following footsteps or the sound of horsemen in pursuit. All I hear is the rain on the leaves, the crack of a dead branch giving way under the weight of water, and my own slow footsteps treading upon twigs and stones. All I see is a long war and death before I have a chance to sire my sons, and all I feel behind me are those same sons trailing my steps upwards, not one or two but many, ranged from youngest to eldest, my scions down the centuries in their thousands. Like the leaves on the trees, drenched and bound to fall.

And now, here is the sound of someone following. One, or more than one? Or none — and it's only my rain-drenched imaginings? But these are footsteps. And the tap of horseshoes on pebbles. My escape is unlikely, my recapture inevitable. I try to think of bold words in my King's honour to say to the crowd that will hiss and shame me at the courthouse, something that will sound loyal. I won't give away my loss of faith in the King who knows we have lost the country but fights on, his little beard pointing gallantly ahead as our sons and brothers fall.

I rise, ready to run on towards Oxford, to rejoin the cause. Or perhaps better down to Calais, in some disguise, to cross the Channel and learn a cheerful European tongue.

But when the horse and rider catch up with me, I see that it's Noble, led by Corianna, wearing her mob cap.

I stand speechless. "I never thought to see you again."

"Nor me." She holds a tightly wrapped bundle of cloth with her free hand; the other has Noble's reins. "So I made myself a wager. If I was right, and you were sitting here sulking, then I would be the cleverest girl in Hertfordshire."

"You always were. I kissed you here once," I tell her. I don't know whether it's true, but it's likely. "Thank you for bringing Noble."

"You're welcome." She hands me Noble's reins and wraps both arms around the bundle of clothes.

I can see that she's waiting for something. I add, "And thank you for helping me escape trial."

She's still waiting, looking idly about her.

"And avoiding hanging, or something like it."

"Hanging, I think, is right."

I stare at her. She stares into the trees and adjusts the bundle slightly.

I ask, "Is there something more I should say?"

"Do you only want the boyhood dream of me, or do you want me as I have become?"

Anything I say will be wrong, so I say nothing.

She looks up at the sky. "In fairness, I ought let you know that you have one more opportunity coming to you. Only one, mind."

I scowl. Should I ask about the sword? No, better not. Or say something more about her lost husband? I've said I'm sorry. Should I be sorrier still? She offers me one chance. Why is nothing fair in this sopping wet world?

I say her name. She turns and I read the question in her bright eyes, her furrowed forehead beneath the married woman's mob cap.

She adjusts the bundle she's holding. Could this be her clothing? Has she packed to travel with me?

"Will you come with me to Oxford?" I ask her. "Will you take off that mob cap and come with me?"

She steps forward. Finally she smiles. I remember the smile, it changes her completely. When she smiles, she's not angry or impatient. She's mine.

She glances down at the bundle of clothing in her arms. "That's not the right question, Spencer."

Hopelessly, and completely outside her rules, I ask anew, "Will you show me what you're holding in your arms?"

She holds out the bundle. "That's the right question."

Noble makes a huffing noise. Corianna is silent. I stare down at a tiny child, wrapped in wool and sleeping soundly.

She gazes down at it. "This is a publican's baby, Spencer."

I was a married woman, Spencer. Use your wooden head. You must know what that means. I say, to give myself a moment, "Beautiful child. Looks just like you."

"His name is Devon. Same as his father."

Now that I see the curve of Devon's cheek, and the curve of his mother's pout on the defenceless sleeping child, I realize that the problem is not so much that he's a publican's child. *He's not mine.* I remember that there are many young women back in Oxford, aristocratic, sweet-faced, and missing their dead husbands and sweethearts. Some are so kind that we've become friends. I need never have left to find a wife. Why, then, did I abandon King and country to return?

I clear my throat. "Will you marry me, Corianna?"

"Spencer, it's still the wrong question."

I throw my arms out wide and turn away. The rain falls down on the three of us, and Noble wanders a little way off, bends his head, and tugs at low greenery. I am here, and I am about to shout at her as I have not shouted at her since we were seven years old. She is still stubborn, still impossible, and now she has another husband's baby. I drop my arms.

"Will you and young Devon marry me, Corianna?"

She scowls. "You can't marry a baby."

I move up close to her. I touch Devon's smooth, damp cheek. "This is your last chance, Corianna. If you're not here simply to dangle before me what can never be, will you give me an answer?"

She pulls Devon away from me. "Here's my question, first. Must you go to war?"

I turn towards Oxford, where the King's army waits. I gaze south, towards the Continent. I say, "Yes, I fear that I do have to go to war."

She sighs. "Will you make at least a half an effort to stay alive?"

"Yes." I take the baby with care, give Corianna a leg up onto Noble's back, and hand the child up to her. I swing into the saddle behind them. We move off at a swaying walk through the trees. I'm sad to think that my sword is back in the well at her father's public house, but where we're going, there are numbers of swords without masters.

"Have you ever been to Oxford?" I wrap my arms around Corianna and the baby.

"No. I've always wanted to go."

"Ah," I say, thinking of the crowds there, the filth and the terrible news from the fighting front each day. "You'll like it, I think. There are lots of books."

She leans back against me. "I think that will be lovely."

By midnight, the white rose moon shines out from deep indigo, and the stars in the sky mirror the white flowers flattened under Noble's hooves.

Chapter Eight

I opened my eyes and looked up at the underside of the willow tree. The sword had fallen onto the ground beside me, between two roots. For a long, magical moment I felt like Merlin, lured into this cave-like space, living backwards through time, and all for love. A buzz rippled nearby along with the canal water, and I realized that my phone had woken me. I sat up, bent over, and reached down to my torn trouser leg. My leg had stopped bleeding.

The phone had stopped buzzing, and now it started up again. A text from Byron showed on the screen. He, Stan, and Eustace were waiting for me at the Old Bearded Lamb, unless I had died of my wound, in which case they were toasting my memory.

I picked up the sword with care for its delicate, rusted condition and carried it towards the Seven Swans, with its gap-toothed roof tiles, sunlit walls, and peeling plaster. There was a single rose climbing up the wall facing the canal. The rose had apparently bloomed while I was under the tree.

I stepped just inside the pub door and set the sword atop the beam that held a battered Tudor-era pewter cup, as a second genuine but entirely unattractive decoration. Once outside again, I looked the old public house right in the eaves. "That

Corianna was a lot more like Holly than anything we've had yet," I said aloud.

No answer, of course, from the Seven Swans. From Corianna, an echo: *Do you only want the boyhood dream of me, or do you want me as I have become?*

And then, without warning or an apparent source: *What now?*

It was a question that I had stopped asking myself at least twenty years earlier.

To be sure, I'd asked a lot of *What next?* since Angelica left me. But not a lot of *What now?* I remembered asking Holly *What, then?* because the question was always arising in the Sufi poems Holly would read to me on a beach in Corfu, her yellow hair fanned out over my knees as she lay in my lap and held up the black exercise book she wrote poetry and Joni Mitchell lyrics in. I remembered the Sufi poems because they were so short, little light puffs of poems so heavy with import that they had endured hundreds of years, the way this pub had endured.

And I remembered one particular Sufi poem because I had laughed at her for it and then apologized for three days before she would lay her head on my lap again and let me run my hands through her hair, while I repeated it from memory to show how enlightened the last three days had made me.

"*What then is all the harvest of this workshop of generation and corruption?*"

And she had said the answer. "*Not much.*"

"*We wait on the lip of the sea of Nothing. O Saki, one cup! What space between lip and cup?*"

"*Not much,*" Holly had answered.

I pulled out the phone again and, keeping my thumbs and fingers as steady as I could manage it, accessed the old Twitter account I'd created when I thought I might write a novel and tweet the sentences one at a time to a world full of patient readers. The novel was about lost love — all novels are about lost love, even the ones about Jack Reacher and his ex-wife, the US Army — and so I knew what hashtag to put in to track down ex-girlfriends from forty years ago.

#lostlove.

And then I typed *#lostlove* and *@HollyW* and *#HollyW* and *What space between lip and cup?*

A moment later the answer arrived to me with a little beep from across the world or down the canal, there was no way to know. It simply said, *Not Much.* And was signed *@HollyW.* And retweeted.

I stared at the phone. And as I did so another beep arrived. *Not much.* From another, *@HollyW.* And another beep. This one read, *Not much motherfucker@angrybloodypoet.*

I was aware that there were many Hollys out there in the greater world, but it was with a hammering heart that I slipped the phone into my back pocket.

§

For Spencer Stevens and the Seven Swans, more adventures, disasters, and victories are ahead. Find him up to his ears in trouble and mystery in Book 4 of the Hertfordshire Pub Mysteries, coming up in Issue 15, Summer 2017.

POETRY

Susie Taylor
Daniel Aristi
Jude Neale
Elizabeth Amerding

These four poems were shortlisted for the 2016 Magpie Award for Poetry. Our poetry editor Daniel Cowper liked them too much to leave them unpublished, and we're happy to agree with him.

Susie Taylor lives and writes in Harbour Grace, Newfoundland. She won the 2015 NLCU Fresh Fish Award for her novel Dispelling the Myths. *Her work has appeared in* Riddle Fence.

The Third Day of Spring

Susie Taylor

There have been suicide bombings in Belgium;
reverberations of despair hitting us on this North Atlantic island.
A description of glass falling on a woman's foot
coming through my radio.
There is a report of an accident on the highway.
Someone is dead and a car burning.
My mother has called to tell me of a suicide in Bear's Cove;
not a drowning, as I imagined first,
but a hanging.
A body found suspended in the rust coloured shed.
And the wind howls and howls and the front door keeps banging in its frame

and the chair and desk I write at shake.
It is the third day of spring and the second day of my period.
Clots of blood are splattered on the bathroom floor
flung from the tampon I pulled out in the night.
This morning I found a bloody hand print on my thigh.
Through my buffeting window I watch as my neighbour smokes.
She stands on her porch in the hundred kilometre gusts.
And I am envious of her,
the fuck you of it:
smoking in the wind.

Daniel Aristi was born in Spain, and he studied French Literature at the French Lycée in San Sebastian. He now lives and writes in Switzerland. Daniel's work is forthcoming in Queen's Ferry Press Anthology 2016, LA Review, Brilliant Flash Fiction *and* Berkeley Poetry Review.

AMAZON

DANIEL ARISTI

Ma'am—

How'd you make love to and not fuck

a Sargent-woman?

I know I shall paint portraits and portraits
And portraits of you
As Pallas Athene
When I retire but, right now, right where the road is exploding
to the sky

I don't feel only the taste of bread in my mouth
When I see you, but something meatier is there as well,
Like corned beef sandwich.

Comrade-in-my-arms
In Babylon.

In your tent, we've pretended you're the Sheikh's daughter.
We lay so close & dog-tag-naked — two fire-ready bullets in
a mag.

Though, would I/you desire you/me
With no legs? This comes up *a lot.*

Today, camouflaged breasts occupy my mind in the Chinook,
like some fable,
Like a gross miscalculation,
Like.

Jude Neale's *poetry has been shortlisted for more than half a dozen international poetry prizes, including our own Magpie Awards in 2014, 2015, and 2016. Her book,* Splendid in its Silence, *has been shortlisted for upcoming publication in the UK.*

About Light

Jude Neale

I could have died on this road alone

but for the fever of your touch.

You pull crusts off my naked loneliness

and lessen this wake I drag
behind me like a stillborn.

You name my doddering illness
that hides in a bucket of shame.

I'm sorry I forget how to think
about light, trapped

curious curled words
clasped in my trembling hands.

I hope you will love me
despite endings

when I don't die with longing,

I don't even die for your lips
to press like wet poppies
onto my white waxen face.

In the end we carry nothing but stones
and skinned knees down to the river.

Bruised and broken we aren't afraid.
We teeter onto one another's empty stage

arms suspended like angels before the fall.

Elizabeth Armerding *lives in Vancouver, BC, and enjoys bikes, condiments, and leaving an unwelcome trail of glitter.*

F/G/C/F
(COUNTRY LOVE SESTINA)

ELIZABETH ARMERDING

Coming up with a country song
must involve a special collection of words.
Recurring content on JRFM: pick-up truck,
cold beer, moonlight, woman, love.
Chart-toppers in the New Country
category always bring up beer.

I never turn down a cold beer.
This is why there are never any in my fridge. Love
is a cold beer, can be the lyrics. I hope you get a truck;
prune beds in some new country,
I'm your girl. No. Only a chorus, I feel sorry for the song.
You used to look to me for words,

and I had about a million; words
about right and wrong, tomato products, love,
bla bla bla, how when living in a different country
they have cheap, delicious beer,
how change is good for a person. Youtube, classic song
featuring good old boys and whiskey. No truck.

Take me on the open road! honks the truck,
hoping to help us write a song
about the future. I say, The Power of Love?
But truck says those are someone else's words,
and anyway, it's pop. Our song must involve beer,
remember, and those other things to make it country.

Wise truck knows real country
is all heart, you can't just wing a song.
No sir. I look to good old truck
(who doesn't exist) for Alabama, beer,
horse, cowboy, any of those words,
and realize I don't know how to love

you, nor you me. Maybe love
to the tender tune of country
could've saved us, but no mention of truck,
we're not good old boys. Not even beer,
home or abroad, can change the words
of our hopeless, half-written country song.

```
F                G
```
Truck and me, we sing a song for country/
```
C               F
```
boots up on the dash / Trade words, crack a beer and
```
G               F                G          C
```
try to remember / love is anywhere you hang your hat.

THE GREEN THREAD AND THE BLUE

Carolyn Oliver

A graduate of The Ohio State University and Boston University, **Carolyn Oliver** *lives in Massachusetts with her family. Her work has appeared in or is forthcoming from* Slush Pile Magazine, Midway Journal, matchbook, *and* Constellations, *among others. This not-quite fairy tale was inspired by her mother. More of Carolyn's writing can be found at carolynoliver.net.*

The Green Thread and the Blue

That's it, dear. You're the first one to learn the way of it in less than a month. My compliments to your mother — how is she? Well, I hope? I heard there's a touch of the summer fever in town. Give me that plait when you've finished. I have some strong thread here to tie it off. One of your predecessors spun it for me — doesn't it sparkle? Like ale in the sunlight, as I recall. She was a canny one. I wish I could remember her name; you could look her up, then.

I can tell you're looking at my hands. That's all right. I believe the word is *gnarled*, like tree roots, the pesky things. Always tripping visitors or trying to roust the foundations of the house. But my hands are not really gnarled. They're snarled.

And that's what I want to talk to you about, dear. No, no, the yarn is fine, and you've done a lovely job with my hair — I can feel how smooth it is. No, that is not what I meant at all. Sit beside me on the bench, just there. You'll feel the indent. I've learned you girls take things easier when you're not looking at me in the eyes. Or where my eyes used to be, I should say.

Now then. You have plaited my hair seventeen times, and for seventeen days, as you've learned my scalp and my wisps of white, I've learned you. I can smell — my sense of smell is very strong — that your dress is dyed with woad, but faintly; you've worn it nine times to visit me, more than any other dress: your favourite, no doubt, because it sets off your raven-black hair and hazel eyes. Yes, your beauty is discussed at the well — did you know? The dress is threadbare at the elbows — second-hand, it would seem. Though it's not from one of your sisters or cousins, since you have none, so it must be a friend's dress. You have friends, then, friends who are no more put off by your beauty than I am, an old eyeless crone. Which means you have personality. And I know you have sense, since you have not spoken a word more than necessary in all your hours here. A wise woman in these days knows not to reveal her thoughts to a stranger. Or her family, for that matter.

And you have courage. I heard about the rescue of the boy in the well, just like everyone else in the village. But I also know what you did for the miller's daughter, getting her to the midwife before it was too late. The miller's daughter has plaited my hair too, and she does not have quite your sense.

You are shifting in your seat, and perhaps you are right to be uncomfortable, to be restless. A girl like you should be going places, seeing things, meeting people, the good and the wicked, yes?

Ah, and there we have it. You are looking now at the mirror on the wall, wondering not at your own beauty but at the mirror's opulence. It doesn't belong in a house like this, you're thinking, and besides, why hasn't some village lad stolen it, sold it off to the goldsmith — who, between us, is not as honest as his face suggests — or spied it through the window, telling his friend, who tells another, and so on until bandits come down from the hills to take it in the night from an old blind woman?

The mirror, like most magic mirrors, has more than one purpose. This one happens to repel men, to keep them away from the house, to answer the question you were too polite to ask. The mirror was a gift from a girl like you. Very like you, in fact: raven hair, lips red as the rose, skin as clear and pale as skimmed milk, but with eyes of deepest blue. You know her name. You know her story: the blood sacrifice of the deer, the hunter, the fruit. All of us do. And once upon a time, when I had eyes, she plaited my hair for many days, and I offered her the choice that will be yours.

I offered a choice to all of them: the girl who spun straw into gold thread, the girl who slept for one lifetime and woke again for another, the girl who walked on knives for love. The one who lost her slipper, the one whose tears melted ice and snow, the great witch-killer with her oven. That oven over there, actually.

And I offered the choice to girls you've never heard of: some homely, some lovely; some very good, some just a bit wicked; some strong and some nimble; some impetuous and some wise. But you do not know their names or their stories any more than you know the way your own course will take you. Nobody else does either, or ever will.

I do not offer the choice to all the girls who come to me; some, like your flour-dusted friend, go home after a few days with a pocketful of gold and tales of my strange house, my terrible face. It's harmless enough. But I learned very long ago, when the world and I were young, not to offer the choice to boys. The damage men can do is difficult to unknit; it's the work of centuries, and not mine alone.

But the church bells are tolling twelve; no doubt you've wool left to card and weeds to pull before this warm afternoon is over. Sometimes I think I really am an old woman, forgetting the way of things. Put your hands out, dear, palms down. Good. Now rest them just under mine, not touching. Close your eyes for a moment, and then open them again.

Don't be alarmed; I told you my hands were snarled. That's what happens, of course, and for hours sometimes I lose feeling in some of the fingers. But one does one's duty, and it does offer a few advantages. The tapestry under your fingers, for example. It only appears to others when I wish, by my invitation. But it is always here — you see how it extends past us, into the other room and out of sight. I have been weaving for a long time, and I am always at work. That's why you girls come to plait my hair; my hands are occupied with these threads. You see the kelp, feel the satin fin of the whale? Perhaps you have wished to visit the sea. There now. Drop those pretty hands, dear, and listen.

If I pull this green thread in my left hand, your life will continue on in the groove that waits for it. Your parents will care for you, will even allow you to go to the market over the mountains you have so longed to see, but you will come back here, and the wool and the weeds will always be waiting. You will love and be loved by friends; the miller's daughter is just the first. You will, perhaps, marry and have children. Whatever takes your life — childbirth, or famine, or sickness, or old age — will take it here, in this village. And you will be missed, for a time.

This is the first choice: a life like the one you know. You understand its price, yes?

I lied a little when I said you did not know the names of those who took the choice. For you know your mother's name, do you not? She chose the green thread.

Now, if I pull this blue thread in my right hand, you will venture to lands you have never imagined, not even in the dreams you had after the spice trader came. You will suffer, as all women suffer, but you will persevere through all dangers, and your triumph will sound through centuries and continents, not merely in the birthing room or the lambing fields or the supper table during a long winter. You will be very poor, and then likely quite rich, either in love or gold or both. As if pulled by an invisible thread, you will come back to this place only once, to bring me my gift and your story.

The price is simple: your mother's life.

You draw back, you recoil. I know the harshness of it. I did not set the price, but the price it is. A mother like yours is protection from danger and opportunity alike. If she had not been gathering mushrooms that day, do you believe you would have been the one to save the boy from the well?

This is the second choice, and if you accept the price, you will have a blessing too: you won't remember that you accepted it. You will leave my house and tomorrow your mother will take ill with that fever going around the village. You will see her grave before your new life begins, and I will see to it that violets bloom around it long after you too are dead.

Will you be happy?

That I cannot say, child, no matter which thread you choose.

But observe the tapestry again, the right side. Smooth, not a single stitch puckered or out of place. Now feel the wrong side: the tangles, the loose thread. There's something there, hmm?

Shapes are coming. Knots of stars, snarls working into the buds of trees, houses rising. Soon it will be peopled.

This is my work, the tangling of chances like yours into a new world. A long, long time from now it will be finished. No more threads to pull, no more prices to pay. But not this afternoon, dear.

Which did I choose? Neither, my child. That is why I weave.

PIANO MUSIC

Susan Pieters

Susan Pieters, *one of* Pulp Literature's *founding editors, is a writer who believes that less is more.*

$\mathcal{P}$IANO MUSIC

She searched, but no online station played the right tunes, the Level 5 Chopin mixed with Disney princess songs that her daughter had practised while she herself scorched dinner, fan on high. She'd not listened then. Now she understood what channel it had been on, and wished she had subscribed.

MERMAIL

Eric Del Carlo

Eric Del Carlo's *fiction has appeared in* Asimov's, Analog, Strange Horizons, *and many other venues. His novels include* The Golden Gate Is Empty, *co-written with his father Victor Del Carlo, and the* Wartorn *series published by Ace Books, co-written with Robert Asprin. Find him on Facebook for comments and questions. Don't be shy.*

Mermail

Sixto Auten had a cop. And having a cop meant he could hear every slosh from the back of the van, amplified by nerves, so that surely the steroid-head in the cruiser four car lengths back also heard the giveaway splashings.

He was creeping through the wharf district. Four-thirty traffic. Good cover. Just had to get to the freeway.

Palms slick on the van's steering wheel ...

The thing was not to look like a smuggle van. But there were differing schools of thought. A van too clean seemed an Easter egg to Sixto; *got* to see what's in it. A broke-down sleaze machine had too much against it already. It might be stopped for normal inspection reasons. And of course you couldn't use anything commercial. The feds were all over the shipping companies.

So, if you wanted to move a mermaid, you had to get the right van and the right driver.

And you had to be lucky.

This wasn't lucky. But Sixto *was* the right driver, or a good driver, anyway. He showed up when and where he was supposed to. He felt the proper amount of fear. The police didn't want him for anything. All he had to do now was get his van through this maze of competing one-way streets and to the on-ramp. On the freeway his windowless van would be just another vehicle racing for parts unknown. The water in the tank could slosh all it wanted. His passenger could float and bob to her senseless heart's content.

He'd been paid half up front, but he needed all the money this job would yield.

Stop signs at every intersection. Jerky forward movement. The cars behind Sixto peeled off. The cop slid in on his back bumper. Plenty of time for him to stare, to wonder what's inside. It *is* the right size for a tankful of water—

Just enough fear kept Sixto sharp without panicking him. He maintained a normal speed on the streets. When he braked, the seawater slapped against the fore of the transparent metaplastic tank. It didn't leak. *That* would be a hell of a giveaway, the van dribbling out a trail for all to see. Might as well slap mermaid smuggling on the sides.

This wasn't Sixto Auten's first run. At twenty-seven, he wasn't quite sure how he'd gotten into this line of work, but it was the only thing bringing him an adequate income in this lousy economy. Simple survival shouldn't be this hard, he thought, but it was. It also shouldn't be so ... morally questionable. A market had been created by the very unexpected phenomenon of the mermaids, and it required appropriate labourers. But he was definitely a landlubber. A ferry ride could make him puke. No hauling the half-fish lovelies out of the ocean for him. When he received them, they were doped out sacks of flesh and scales.

His driving gogs gave him a rearview window in the left lens. Sunlight flashed on and off the windshield of the cop car as it slanted between buildings. The policeman had a thick neck, one hand dangling casually out the driver's side window. From what little Sixto could tell, he didn't appear interested in the van. But he could blurp that siren at any second, out of instinct or boredom.

That freeway on-ramp was coming up.

Sixto rolled up to the final intersection, a traffic light. Water softly and heavily smacked the front of the tank. And ... there seemed another sound. A deliberate splash, or bubbles breaking. Some noise that indicated a concentrated activity. Suddenly a terrible itch sprang up between Sixto's protruding shoulder blades. A primal intuition wanted him to turn around. But the cop could be watching him on the intersection's cameras. He needed to maintain a nonchalant demeanour. Drivers of semi-suspicious vans in this city's waterside district had to appear absolutely innocent of all wrongdoing.

He gripped the wheel, watched the lights cycle, watched the police cruiser in his left lens.

Green light. He headed up the ramp, accelerating. Going inland, away from the mermaid's home waters.

It was a crime new to the marketplace of police procedures. The cops, like Sixto and his ilk, were still adjusting, fine-tuning. It was smuggling, yes; but it was also kidnapping—sort of. There wasn't even a pop cultural term for the illegal undertaking yet.

By the time Sixto had a view of the warehouse, he'd also put himself in sight of the police carnival surrounding the place.

Here was where he could prove himself a *good* driver, not just an adequate, show-up-on-time one. He kept going along the uneven, ill-lit street. He rolled up to the seedy warehouse, which, frankly, *looked* like a smuggling stash house, an urban pirate cave.

Civilian vehicles were being directed away from the scene of spinning red lights and milling uniforms. Sixto was the only one driving a van, and here, outside the drop-off point, the vehicle looked so conspicuous, so blatant.

He eased into the crush of police on the street outside the warehouse. He rolled down his window and knocked on the van's door for attention. An officer in a canary slicker — it had rained earlier — stepped toward him, a clouded look on her face.

If the police had laid an ambush, they could have picked off smugglers bringing in their loads one at a time. Sixto didn't imagine for a second he was the only driver who'd been directed to this inland city's dingy commercial district.

"Yo!" Sixto called, because that was the most obnoxious salutation he could think of. He leaned out the window, still hearing the water settle in the tank behind his seat.

"'Yo' what?"

"Where the fuck is 1488 J? I've been circling this shitty neighbourhood for half an hour, looking for the fourteen hundred block. Can't you people put some goddamn street signs up?"

She didn't like his tone, didn't like *him*. That was good. It would distract her from any other considerations.

She had steely eyes under her cap's black brim. "What do your gogs tell you?"

He still had on his driving goggles. Stupid — although maybe it would have looked odd if he hadn't been wearing them, since most everyone did. With sour impatience he said, "They say J Street is here. But apparently 1488 is just some kind of myth, since I can't find anything past seven hundred something — "

"That's because it's *West* J Street on this side of town, moron. Turn left and go two miles, and if you can't find it, you probably shouldn't be allowed to operate a vehicle."

She was three strides from his open window. The scent of saltwater filled his nostrils.

He heaved a terribly dramatic sigh, said with acute sarcasm, "Thanks *so* much!" and turned the van, leaving the compromised warehouse behind.

He had thought clearly, acted quickly, and had had the foresight to study the city's layout beforehand. A good driver, yes. But none of that answered the dire quandary he now faced ...

What to do with his mermaid.

Finding a landline was like trying to locate a telegraph office. But it was the last means of unmonitored communication in this country. Supposedly. Maybe that was an urban myth. At any rate, he'd been pointedly instructed never to phone the number they'd nonetheless given him. And if he did phone in an emergency, which he never should, for chrissake use a landline.

He found a sleazebag motel, got a room, and punched numbers into a chunky mechanical thing that plugged into the baseboard.

The voice that answered on the second ring was measured and pleasant, a receptionist's tone. Sixto had been told code names, but he'd forgotten half of them. He remembered enough to identify himself. Someone else came on. A guarded, tense voice.

Sixto didn't know who he was working for. He'd only met with intermediaries of intermediaries. That was how this new trade worked. It probably kept the top people insulated, but it made for lots of moving parts. One of those had failed, and now the warehouse — likely a hub for the operation — was seized.

The person plainly knew what had happened. He told Sixto, "There's no alternate site, understand? You can walk. Or … something else. Up to you. Make direct delivery. You want that location?"

Sixto, with the stupid heavy earpiece pressed to his head, sorted through the cryptic talk-arounds. *You can walk.* He was being given permission to abandon the run. It would mean forgoing the back half of his payment, which wouldn't leave him enough to get him through rent and bills. What the suggestion also implied, of course, was dumping his cargo. Where? Find a saltwater lake this far inland? No. Just toss her out, anywhere. A roadside, a dumpster.

He had barely looked at the creature in his tank. She was still doped up. But the notion, the very possibility, of heaving it — *her* — out like a load of garbage tightened his tissues and curdled his spirit. It was one thing to smuggle, even living beings. It was something else to have a direct hand in their deaths. His moral compass didn't point that way.

Into the telephone he said, "Give me the location."

It was in code, but a simple letter replacement cryptogram which he was able to remember. The point of ultimate delivery was several states away. He had a lot of driving ahead.

Hearse drivers must occasionally wonder if their charges are sitting up in the casket, watching them with dead, baleful eyes.

At the start of this run, as with every run he'd done, Sixto had received a loaded hypo. If the mermaid woke up — and this would *never* happen, he was assured — he could plunge her with this stuff and knock her back out. He didn't know what the syringe contained. He didn't know where he supposed to inject her. In the arm? On her fish butt?

What he did know was that if things had gone according to plan, he would have delivered her to the warehouse, drained and broken down his metaplastic tank, and been driving back to his apartment on the coast by now without fear of police inquiry.

So he might need to give her the shot.

He rolled the van behind some night-dark trees. With the windows cracked he could smell the pines. He snapped on the overhead light and took his first good long look in a hundred miles at the occupant of the seawater-filled tank.

The mermaid lay facedown. With the water still settling, her limbs were slightly adrift. She had very dark hair, probably shoulder-length if she were upright and out of the water. Her skin was a rich olive. She had sound muscle tone. Her breasts were small, the nipples erect. In adolescence, Sixto Auten had never decided if he liked girls more than boys, and had finally settled for default bisexuality like most everybody did in school nowadays.

But he had to admit, as he peered into the tank from several angles, the mermaid had a very attractive body. The upper half, anyway ...

He kept himself to the task at hand. She was breathing. He could see her gills work. But was she near consciousness? The tank was open; he could reach in—

Again something instinctive seized him. Just as he couldn't toss her out, he couldn't grope—or even nudge—her while she was narcotized. The mermaid was just too *other*. He didn't even like the idea of jabbing the hypo into her shoulder. But he couldn't have her awake for this unexpectedly extended trip.

At some point during this study and musing, he had taken up the syringe. He gazed at her a moment longer. It was easy to say the goldfish in your bowl weren't suffering. Look at them dart about, they're eating, their water is clean. Less easy to tell yourself an adult-sized half-human was perfectly content to lie insensate in a vat of seawater in the back of a moving van.

There was a foot and a half gap between the top of the tank and the roof of the van. He reached over and stuck in the needle. A thread of blood curled from the entry point. It thinned quickly, but not before Sixto saw it was unnervingly, and familiarly, red. He had never seen one of the creatures bleed before.

The predawn sky looked like sickly flesh, and his head felt cottony from lack of sleep and insufficient food. That was when an unbidden message appeared in his driving gogs.

YOU DON'T HAVE TO DO THIS.

For half a heartbeat he thought it was pure hallucination, but it *was* the goggles' font, the words floating out ahead at a comfortable reading distance, translucent so as not to interfere with his driving.

But the message made no sense. It certainly wasn't any kind of traffic advisory.

Sixto's eyes hurt too badly to pick out a reply on a virtual keyboard. He tapped the left temple for voice interface.

"I don't have to do what?" He was hoarse, and annoyed, and in need of a break from his travels.

THE MERMAID IS AN INNOCENT CREATURE. YOU DON'T HAVE TO DELIVER HER INTO CRIMINAL HANDS.

He hit the brakes, too hard. Behind, water sloshed violently. He winced as he heard a dull thump on the tank's wall. But he didn't lose his head. He had no traffic behind him. He almost pulled into a small, gravelly cut-out, but instead accelerated.

This road had been rising and dipping through the mountains for hours.

"Who is this?" he asked in a collected manner, though his composure couldn't be translated by the goggles' recognition software. Still, it kept *him* focused.

WE ARE INTERESTED IN THE WELFARE OF YOUR PASSENGER. JUST AS YOU MUST BE.

Sixto was stone-faced. He absorbed the "we," along with the other critical implications of the new message. Smuggling had been easier when all he'd had to worry about was being arrested.

"You're not the police. How can you threaten me?"

NOT THREATENING. APPEALING TO YOUR HUMANITY.

"You hacked my gogs. You got that kind of reach, why not come get me?" No sense in playing guiltless. They knew him.

It was hard to read anything into a pause from a pair of driving goggles, but the lag following his question encouraged Sixto. Maybe he could talk his way out of this somehow.

WE DON'T HAVE THE RESOURCES TO COME GET YOU. IT'S OUR HOPE YOU WILL DO THE RIGHT THING.

Further encouragement. He stayed straight on the empty road. The silhouetted trees were gaining colour with the arriving day. "What do you think the right thing is?"

WE WANT TO GUIDE YOU TO A PLACE WHERE THE MERMAID WILL BE PROTECTED, WHERE NO ONE WILL EXPLOIT HER.

"You might be the competition. I should just hand over my cargo?"

WE ARE NOT SMUGGLERS OR CRIMINALS. WE ARE ACTIVISTS WHO WISH WHAT IS BEST FOR HER.

"Then turn me in to the cops." He said it like a taunt. For the first time since this startling contact, he felt a little surge of confidence. The police could easily box him in on this two-lane. These hackers plainly knew exactly where he was.

THE SO-CALLED AUTHORITIES ARE NOT TO BE TRUSTED EITHER. THEY DON'T OFFER PROPER PROTECTION FOR THESE CREATURES.

So they wouldn't sic the police on him. Great. But how else could they hamper him?

"Who says I'm taking her anyplace she'll be harmed?" It was sophistry, but he needed more info on these people.

WE KNOW WHERE YOU ARE GOING. THE PERSON YOU ARE SUP-POSED TO DELIVER HER TO IS A CRIMINAL MOGUL.

Maybe they'd hacked the motel phone, found out about him, and decoded the address he'd gotten. These were talented hackers.

"Criminal moguls can't take good care of a mermaid?" He imagined some rich Mafioso clown who wanted the creature as a living trophy, something to swim around in a pool and impress friends and associates. Was that a bad life?

MERMAIDS ARE SENTIENT AND INTELLIGENT. YOUR PASSENGER DESERVES A PROTECTED BUT NATURAL LIFE, WHICH WE CAN PROVIDE. AGAIN, WE APPEAL TO YOUR SENSE OF HUMANITY.

Sixto at last allowed himself a smile. They couldn't get to him, and they weren't going to send the police. If he kept burning up the road, he could reach his destination in about thirty hours.

He tossed aside the goggles and rubbed one eye, then the other. He shook his head and straightened up in the seat. One way or the other, he had an ordeal ahead, but he was determined to see this run through.

He had to hit a recharge station, where he also picked up some doses of Stay Awake. His joints ached in a way that told him being twenty-seven wasn't like being seventeen. There wasn't any joy in having stayed up all night, and no giddy anticipation about facing the prospect again so soon. He was going to be a wreck when all this was over, but you had to practically kill yourself to make a living these days anyway.

Still, he'd have fulfilled his obligations. He had to admit this trip was about more than the money. Professional responsibility was involved. He had never been good at anything. Let his skinny ass at least do this thing to the best of his abilities.

He stood looking at the rear of his road-dusty van in the noontime. He had come out of the mountains onto parched flats. Other vehicles came and went at the recharge station and attached mart. He watched them dully but warily. Whenever anybody even glanced at his rig, his heart rate jumped. He had never driven a smuggled load this far. It felt like every mile increased exponentially the possibility of getting caught.

As he waited, a car rolled onto the parking lot from the highway and took the slot next to his van. It was a beat-up roadster with bumper stickers on its backside reading MERMAIDS ARE PEOPLE and PROTECT OUR AQUATIC SISTERS. Sixto's pulse suddenly thumped hard enough he could feel it at his temples.

Maybe the activists had played him. Maybe they did have the manpower to reach him.

He was frozen for several awful seconds, hating himself for his inability to act.

The car sat silently, then its doors opened and a passel of collegiate-looking youngsters piled out rambunctiously and headed into the mart, all the while ignoring Sixto and his van.

He went to disconnect from the charging pylon. As he backed out of the station, he looked at his unconscious passenger. He wondered if she would find comfort in the support of those college kids for her people; then he wondered where the hell that thought had come from.

The Stay Awake gave the desert over-bright details that could distract him from more general, and perhaps more dangerous, features on the road. It also heightened his awareness of the creature floating in the tank just behind his seat. With every slosh he was sure she was stirring into consciousness. What would he do then? He'd had only the single hypo load of tranquilizer.

Urgency, paranoia, and a final fatal fatigue which was gathering at a molecular level and which must eventually overcome him, despite the speedy stuff he'd taken: those were the states he had to deal with as he aimed his van across the numbing wasteland.

Had to finish this run, *had* to—

A billboard came up. The road was arrow-straight, traffic sparse. Sixto's gaze flicked tightly toward the sign . . . which was where he saw his own name.

The oversized LCD surface rippled with the sinuous movements of a cartoon mermaid, a chaste, big-eyed thing right out of Disney. It swam across the billboard, coming to rest at one end. The trail of bubbles quickly formed into words: SIXTO AUTEN, PLEASE KEEP ME SAFE. And those long-lashed eyes blinked as she gave him a plaintive look, turning her head to follow as his van shot past.

He swerved in his lane, overcompensating as he tried to straighten out. His tires squealed, and for a heart-pounding instant he thought he was going spin out. But he wrangled his vehicle.

Had he really seen that? Of course he had! The activists still knew where he was. Their hacking talents were astonishing. He didn't believe they had paid for that billboard. Had any other motorists seen it? Could some deductive driver have spotted his van and made the connection? Were there any Highway Patrol around?

The paranoiac fit was intense. He desperately wanted to pull off the road, but somehow restrained himself. The day was finally beginning to wane. He just had to drive through the night and make it till midday tomorrow. He could do it. He could.

The mermaids, who a year ago had appeared swimming a couple of longitudes between Hawaii and the California coast, had gone from hoax to verified fact in a Grover's Mill minute. They were real, though that "real" was also open to inflammatory debate. Yes, they were flesh and scale beings, living; but where in the *fuck* had they come from? Why were there only females? Had they erupted en masse from an ocean trench? Were they an elaborate — and monumentally expensive — bioengineered prank?

The night beat on the sides and roof of Sixto's van. He couldn't handle another of the chalky blue Stay Awake tablets and so had grabbed a go cup of coffee, which he'd puked up afterward like he was on a whaling ship in stormy weather.

Now he just hung on to the wheel in a death grip. His lower back was a special agony he had never experienced before. It felt like he'd been broken in half and welded back together by a drunken monkey. His vision swam with icy motes. His head ached ferociously. Also, he stank like a hobo.

Behind him, the water splashed.

He didn't stop driving, but glanced sharply and repeatedly until he saw her move in the tank. It was just a spasmodic action, though. Her fishtail flicked the surface, like someone's foot jerking in sleep. She stayed facedown in the water.

The government had declared mermaids a protected species, probably not knowing what else to do about the seaborne oddities. Private citizens, however, wanted to experience these fanciful beings. Humans liked pets and menageries. People with money willing to subvert the law wanted their own specimens.

The feds weren't doing a great job of protecting the mermaids. But it went further, maybe. The activist who'd hacked his goggles had said the authorities couldn't be trusted any better than the criminals. Was the government culling its own specimens from the sea, sending them off to labs to be studied? Surely the creatures *had* to be understood. Science wouldn't allow them to exist without explanation. Maybe the human/fish beings had military applications. Even if they didn't possess wholesale intelligence, perhaps they could be trained like dolphins in underwater combat.

Sixto didn't dwell on it. He was a driver. So he drove, with the last shreds of his strength and lucidity, taking his charge to her new destiny as a crime lord's pet.

The desert became less desert-y, took on scrubland characteristics then real greenery, then it was a whole other region. Sixto turned off the highway and went deeper into the countryside.

He was a wisp of himself. But now that he was on the final leg, vitality returned to him — or a pale, fragile version of it. He could reach his destination.

These were upscale rural tracts. Monied people kept homes here and kept them well, because they could afford the isolation. Sixto guided his van past estates with expansive grounds.

Several times during the last hour he'd heard splashes from the tank. The mermaid was starting to move, perhaps even of her own deliberate volition. But he was minutes away from no longer being her chauffeur or transporter, or whatever the hell the term would be when his particular enterprise reached mass cultural awareness and entered the nomenclature.

The address was just ahead. He rolled toward it. A gate was backed by screening trees which nonetheless let him see the big house's soaring turrets. A goddamn castle. Fine. She would live in a castle, then. Fairy tale ending for a fairy tale creature who probably shouldn't even be a part of this world. If her people had had any sense, they would've stayed myths.

He slowed and stopped. He literally couldn't remember the last time the van had stood motionless. Dazed, he just sat there. The brass gate bore a tacky monogram, like from an ancient gangster movie: NM, presumably the initials of the supposed mogul. With smarting eyes he looked around for a bell, an intercom, something …

With a flurry of motion that was over before he was fully aware of it, a gleaming retro sedan pulled in tightly behind him, chirping its tires. Car doors opened, and fast footfalls followed. Still in his stupor, Sixto felt more than saw a shadow fall across him as someone stepped up to his window.

"Why're you here?" asked a deep voice.

Sixto blinked at the central casting goomba next to the van who was blocking out the midday sun. For a second he felt a laugh come on, a real hysterical jag, but he reined it in and spoke his code name very, very clearly. Someone else was standing on the van's passenger side, and that person may or may not have been holding a weapon.

Everything was hazy and twirly. The deep voice had said something.

"Huh?" asked Sixto.

The goomba didn't like that, but he repeated, "She in there?" He wore sunglasses, but Sixto managed to catch the flick of his gaze past Sixto's shoulder.

"Yeah ..."

The big man stepped back and spoke into a phone. Sixto heard nothing until, after a lengthy pause, the man said, "Yes, Mr Martorello."

Then he had returned to Sixto's open window. The van still idled. Distantly, Sixto heard a watery sound, possibly followed by a thump, as of a limb against the tank wall.

"Where you want her?" he asked, feeling a ridiculous dreamy smile on his lips.

The goomba frowned, maybe thinking Sixto was stoned or just unprofessional. Sixto didn't care. He didn't give a rat's ass. This was almost over! The bodyguard said, "Follow the drive round back. Boss wants her in the guest house ... right away." Sixto didn't see him use a device, but the brass gate parted to reveal the cobbled drive, bordered by a profusion of chrysanthemums.

The two goons returned to the sedan. They were plainly escorting him onto the grounds.

Right away. The gorilla had leered when he'd said that, just subtly. Even in his present condition Sixto hadn't missed it. But the implications were only now setting in.

Boss. Guest house. Right away.

Not a pet to swim in a pool or oversized aquarium. Humans were curious about these new creatures. That included sexual curiosity.

Ever want to fuck a mermaid?

Behind, he heard a thrashing. Warm saltwater flecked the back of his neck. Sixto put the van in drive and started forward onto the mogul's estate. He kept a sedate speed. The house ahead was massive. The sedan crept along, right on his tail.

Something broke the surface of the tank, displacing a volume of water. It was accompanied by a great sucking inhalation. Mermaids could breathe both water and air. It was how this kingpin would be able to interact with the object of his curiosity.

He wouldn't be a party to her death. But could he stand to contribute to . . . *this* unwholesome fate for her?

The deep inhale was followed by a raw, frightened mewl.

Sixto slammed down on the accelerator and spun the wheel. Chunks and tatters of violated chrysanthemums flew up against the windshield. He cut a tight circle around the sedan and raced for the gate, which was swinging shut.

He lost a sideview mirror going out, but he was on the country road again, tearing along at high speed. It would take a few seconds for the gate to cycle open again. He had studied a map of the area beforehand because he was a good driver, so the layout was no mystery to him. An interstate and two major highways were within reach. That sedan had looked elegant and vaguely sinister, but he doubted it was built for velocity. Even so, he pushed his rig as fast as he dared.

When he was on a multi-laned roadway once again, he dropped in among the many other anonymous travellers.

It wasn't until then that he picked up his driving goggles from the passenger seat, where he'd discarded them early the day before. The voice interface was still activated.

"So, where am I taking her?"

There was a lull. Nothing. Maybe they'd given up on him. Then—

WE ARE SO HAPPY YOU HAVE CHANGED YOUR MIND.

Directions followed. He was going to have to get off this road and turn north. He made for an exit lane. He would get some distance, then pull off and grab some sleep. He was far enough inland by now that a van wouldn't arouse automatic suspicion from the police. Certainly, though, today's stunt would end his career as a smuggler. But maybe this wouldn't be his only run for the activists, if they indeed had the means to protect the waterborne creatures. He could apply his talents there and be a part of that movement, whatever it was called. The Undersea Railroad? No, too heavy. Maybe something cheekier, a play on words …

He slowed at the end of the off-ramp and turned around in his seat. The mermaid's head was out of the water. Wet hanks of hair fell across her face. She reached out a hand and touched his cheek with soft fingertips. And she spoke. It was a strange mixture of sound. Some impossible blend of dolphin whistling and mammalian grunts, underscored with odd, beautiful musical notes.

He smiled with vast weariness. The movement of facial muscles made her fingers drag at the stubble on his cheeks. "What are you saying?" he wondered aloud, liking her touch, liking her face.

SHE IS TELLING YOU HER NAME. SHE IS ALSO SAYING SHE IS SCARED.

Was that really language? Had the activist group interacted enough with the beings to decipher it?

He touched her hand. "My name is Sixto Auten. And you don't have to be afraid anymore."

HOW TO LOSE A WEEK

F J Bergmann

FJ Bergmann frequents a remote fastness in Wisconsin from where she writes poetry and speculative fiction, often simultaneously. She is the editor of Star*Line, *the journal of the Science Fiction Poetry Association (sfpoetry.com) and the poetry editor of* Mobius: The Journal of Social Change *(mobiusmagazine.com). Her work has been published in* Analog, Apex, Dreams & Nightmares, Lakeside Circus, Spectral Realms, *and a bunch of regular literary journals that should have known better. 'Opening Doors' appeared in* Pulp Literature *Issue 6, and we couldn't resist this delicious (if you like calamari) offering from her.*

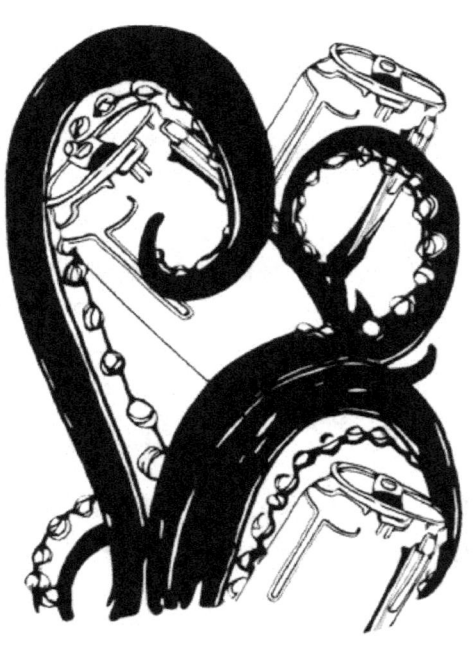

How to Lose a Week

Monday

After accidentally pouring reconstituted orange juice instead of milk into the remaining half-cup of coffee, you make a snap decision that it's okay to go to the art museum instead of work, since you are late to work anyway. When your car won't start because someone who shall not be named left the interior light on, you decide to hitchhike downtown. The eighteen-wheeler that picks you up is going to Florida; you decide that's even more okay. You spend the rest of the day travelling south and taking notes for future use in a roman-à-clef while the trucker tells you his *very* interesting life story. He talks a lot faster than you are used to.

Tuesday

In the wee hours, somewhere near Atlanta, Georgia, the trucker, who has become progressively more wild-eyed and chatty and for some reason hasn't needed to stop for anything but gas, informs you that an alien spaceship is landing on the road ahead, and then he climbs over the back of his seat, screaming, "The tentacles! The tentacles!" You hastily grab the steering wheel. With his foot off the gas, the truck gradually decelerates and you are able to steer it onto the shoulder, where it coasts to a stop, and you turn off the ignition. You are unable to persuade the whimpering truck driver to uncurl from a foetal position, so you decide to walk to a nearby exit, taking the truck's keys with you to prevent any unfortunate incidents. Halfway to the exit ramp, the aliens wave their tentacles at you and one calls out (in a shrill voice with a British accent), "Need a ride, luv?"

The aliens are going to Florida too! They want to see Disney World, which their travel agent recommended. They got lost and stopped to look at the road signs. It figures; their map is twenty-two years old. They seem puzzled that you can tell them where to go even though you are older than the map and even though you have never been to Disney World.

When you get to Disney World, it turns out the aliens have no money (the travel agent had suggested they use the employees' entrance). Luckily, you have credit cards. Also luckily, they are short enough to get child rate tickets. There are not enough of them to merit family rate.

They are crazy about caffeinated soda and cotton candy. Pretty soon they are talking almost as fast as the truck driver. They throw up on every single ride, but it doesn't bother them one bit. The blue skies are cloudless and it's sunny and warm and nice, and you wish you had shorts and a T-shirt and flip-flops, at least until you realize how corrosive the aliens' stomach acids are.

At sunset their eyes begin to emit tiny green sparks, and they reluctantly agree to go back to the spaceship. They are waddling a lot more slowly, and you have to carry two of them. You are almost sure there are fewer of them than you came in with, but they don't seem to care.

The aliens decide to spend the night on a beach. They have heard of jellyfish, but don't really believe in them. Their ship cruises along the coastline while they argue about where to land. You see a bar with 'Tropical Drinks' in blinking neon. It is a very noisy bar, and you suggest that right next to the bar would be a good place to park. You have to explain what a bar is, but they are quite interested, especially after you explain alcohol.

The bar is extremely crowded even though the band, Pooter Squat, is the worst and loudest you have ever heard. It is easy to get drinks because the aliens say they will have whatever you are having (pineapple-mango daiquiris). After the third round, the aliens try to dance, which results in lots of people buying them drinks, which is a good thing because your credit cards are almost maxed out. Their dancing is drawing attention to the point where you are able to lift several wallets from oblivious bar patrons and extract the contents. Some of those guys have *lots* of cash.

At closing time the band's lead singer, who has been drinking gin rickeys (seven of them, by your count), tries to hit on one of the aliens, and you take him along to the ship. It turns out they *do* have rectal probes, but he seems to enjoy it.

WEDNESDAY

The aliens natter on about wanting to meet jellyfish. After dropping the still-comatose lead singer, Bobo, back at his motel (they speak of returning in a few weeks to see how the grubs are maturing) and getting breakfast at a diner, you suggest that they head for the Keys. Earlier, you had presented the aliens with the truck keys as a valuable Earth ceremonial artefact, hoping that they would reciprocate with something interesting, so they are a bit confused until you show them the map again. They become excited upon finding that the shapes of the islands in the archipelago spell out a *very* naughty word indeed in their own language. The word is unfortunately untranslatable, even into French. You explain that the Keys may no longer be exactly the same shapes. You then explain about sand and erosion and tides and storms. They have a lot of trouble believing in weather, especially when you mention hurricanes.

The aliens do a high-altitude flyover of the Keys and the steep ascent makes your ears pop eight times. They are ridiculously disappointed to discover that the islands' shapes no longer spell anything at all. They huddle at the feet (at the lower tentacles, actually) of the ship's computer avatar and seem to argue with it, while you unsuccessfully look for a refrigerator or mini-bar somewhere on board. The ship's big monitor screen shows them some photos of the moon. *A* moon, anyway, and then a bunch of moving spiral patterns overlaid on an aerial view of the Keys. They seem to come to an agreement, and the ship heads away from the Keys, fast. You ask if they can stop somewhere for lunch where you can order lobster, seeing as how you've got all this money from last night, but they ignore you.

You spend the rest of the day zigzagging all over who knows where—all you can see is open ocean. When you ask what they're doing, the aliens tell you the ship is extruding weather parameter modifications. You suggest going to SeaWorld in

Orlando, but they ignore you some more. Sulking, your stomach rumbling, you go to sleep on the floor of a main passageway.

Thursday

Apparently the aliens folded you up while you slept and put you in a closet out of the way. Up on a shelf, in fact, which you discover when you push the door open. They are not good folders, either. The ship is still zooming around over the ocean, but the sky is clouding up, which is annoying since you still had hopes of talking them into going to SeaWorld—and buying yourself swimming attire first. You are sure people would buy you drinks more often if you had a tan.

After you have a bit of a hissy fit, they finally agree to take you to a restaurant in Miami. They say it will take the ship a while to generate a replacement for the broken viewscreen anyway.

They set the ship down on a beach again. Because it has clouded over and begun to rain, it is not too hard to find an empty spot. You all take a taxi into town. The taxi driver does not speak English. The aliens talk to him in their language and laugh hysterically when he answers in his own (Farsi). This makes the driver mad, and he stops the cab and yells at all of you. You get out hastily when he pulls a gun from under the front seat. You are almost downtown, anyway. One of the aliens makes a rude gesture just before you turn a corner. At least you assume it's a rude gesture. So does the cabdriver, who fires a shot at you and misses.

The first two restaurants will not let you in because you do not meet their dress requirements, but the third is not very busy and the maitre d', frankly, does not seem to care. You order lobster and (by request) pineapple-mango daiquiris for everybody. You are very hungry and thirsty because you haven't had anything since Wednesday morning. The lobsters finally come just as you are finishing your third daiquiri. You don't remember anything after the fourth one.

FRIDAY

When you fall out of the closet this time, it is raining so hard you can actually hear it on the spaceship's hull. The aliens are grumpy because the new viewscreen is not finished yet. They say they would consider going to the Miami Seaquarium but they do not want to walk in that much rain — they are still regenerating the integument melted by yesterday's precipitation, they say. You tell them to go ahead and land the spaceship on the aquarium roof; what the heck.

It turns out you *can* get inside from the roof, but you end up in the maintenance areas, so everything is kind of yucky, and there is junk and buckets of dead fish and goop everywhere. You can also lean right over the tanks and reach in and fool around. One of the aliens tries to pet the alligators. And then there is an incident at the shark tank. They act like it's hilarious. Pretty soon all of them are missing part of at least one tentacle, and they are getting rowdier by the minute.

The aliens get intercepted twice by indignant staff, but they certainly know how to use duct tape! When they get to the jellyfish tanks, they're in ecstasy. Most of the jellyfish are pretty small and look like sandwich Baggies, but the aliens are really impressed with the Portuguese man o' war if their shrieking is anything to go by. Then they find a stick that looks like it was meant to be a shark prod and start popping all the jellyfish float bladders. Sort of like you do with bubble wrap.

You try to distract them. "Look! Here's a squid!" They crowd around to look at it. There is a sudden hush when it unfurls its tentacles.

"This ... is *squid*?" one of them says quietly.

"Well, one of 'em, yeah," you answer. "Speaking of which, I could use some lunch sometime real soon; how about you guys?"

They ignore you, and then one of them spots an empty bucket. Before you can tell them that those things have *teeth*, an alien reaches in, grabs the squid, and sets it, writhing gently, in the bucket. It starts slithering out, but another of them speaks to it in a squeaky voice and it settles back down. You swear you can hear a faint chirping from the bucket in response, and the aliens pour in some water for it. After some more high-pitched back-and-forth discussion with the squid, they grab some more buckets, dumping their contents, and filch all the rest of the squid in the aquarium. You'd think squid'd be hard to catch, but those suckers come right up to the top and wait. Some are so eager they are already climbing out over the rims of their tanks. They examine an octopus for several minutes, but finally decide to leave it where it is. Of course, *you* have to carry the two heaviest buckets.

Back at the ship, the aliens install the buckets, with their residents, below the now-replaced viewscreen and all of them watch it intently. It shows an aerial view of the Keys again, but from higher up, and this time part of the spiralling overlay is far too reminiscent of a hurricane to be anything else. "Look, guys," you say nervously, "I don't know how well your spaceship is anchored, or how it handles in 150-mile-an-hour winds, but you might want to go somewhere else for the next few days. I hear there's a nice aquarium in Baltimore. Or how about Chicago?"

Chicago it is. By the time you get there, the Shedd Aquarium is closed, but the aliens nod when you suggest having dinner and getting an early start tomorrow. The Palmer House restaurant doesn't have any problem with your attire, but it also doesn't have pineapple-mango daiquiris, to everyone's sorrow. You are consoled by strawberry margaritas — on an empty stomach, as is becoming habitual; the steaks arrive only after the second pitcher of margaritas has been emptied. You seem to remember several more pitchers arriving.

SATURDAY

Falling out of the closet is also becoming habitual, but for variety you're accompanied by an empty 16-ounce margarita glass, which breaks when you land on it. Cursing, you limp to the ship's bridge (foyer, drawing room, whatever). The squid have mysteriously disappeared, but the empty buckets are ready for more occupants.

"I don't think they'll let you in with those, you guys," you say. It turns out they were planning on the roof approach again. You talk them into going in the normal way and scoping out the place first.

They get a major kick out of the sea snakes, and they go crazy over the poison dart frogs. By the time you leave that part of the exhibit, they have all changed their skin colours to match the frogs: cobalt blue with black polka dots, bright red with black splotches, emerald green, golden yellow, orange, turquoise, even metallic colours. Nobody else notices, as usual. They try all the doors marked 'Employees Only' and crane their necks (or whatever) and squint along the glass walls, trying to see what's on the other side of the tanks. When you finally leave, they look smugly pleased.

Everything is fine until you go out for dinner: an Italian restaurant this time. The aliens are now interested in trying "different Earth food" and are asking the waiter to explain each item on the menu. They have finished with the wine list and are working their way through the appetizers, and it's going smoothly until they reach 'calamari'.

"Um ... it's a deep-sea fish," the waiter says.

"Squid," you say, without thinking. There is a long, deadly silence—and then they all start shrieking at once and waving their tentacles.

"I'll come back for your order, people," the waiter says hastily. "Can I freshen up anyone's drink?"

"Yes," you say, gesturing at your empty glass. The aliens briefly stop the recriminations among themselves to glare at you. "Make it a double—and keep 'em coming."

Sunday

You vaguely remember being shoved down the ramp to land painfully sprawled on the sidewalk outside your house, clutching a doggie bag of leftover lasagna. All the cash is gone, for some reason, and so are your credit cards (much good will *those* do them). You end up sleeping most of the day, occasionally waking briefly to take more Tylenol, put a fresh ice pack on your head, and try to figure out if your rectum feels any different than it did before. In the late afternoon, you decide that some coffee might help.

You finally stagger into the living room and turn on the TV. On the evening news, the devastation wrought by Hurricane Melinda (which happens to be the name of your maternal great-aunt) has displaced any coverage of political events. In particular, they show satellite views of the Florida Keys, whose coastlines have been altered by wind and waves into dramatically new contours. You wonder what *that* word means.

THE HUMMINGBIRD
FLASH FICTION PRIZE

THE 2016 HUMMINGBIRD PRIZE FOR FLASH FICTION

Much as the ruby-throated hummingbird migrates north in the spring, so do expertly faceted narrative gems wing their way to our inboxes to mark the start of this season of revival and rebirth. Many of the entries in our third annual Hummingbird contest were stunning, making the judging process fairly difficult this year. Luckily, we were once again fortunate enough to be joined by award-winning flash fiction author, Bob Thurber. Here is what Bob had to say about the finalists:

Nice job, all of you. A superior batch of finalists. I enjoyed so many of them. Here are my final selections:

Winner
'Xuefei and his heart' by Rebecca Wurtz
for its solid writing and wonderfully intriguing surreality

Runner-up
'Painted Nails' by Jenna Park
for its painful voice and understatement

Honourable Mention
'Scathed' by Holly Woodward
for its wild energy and insistence

And as always with these contests, the senior editors indulge themselves by honouring an additional story that caught their eyes. Here is our selection for Hummingbird 2016:

Editor's Pick
'Better Watch Out' by Anna Belkine
for its wry humour and satirical treatment of North American culture

Our thanks to Bob Thurber for his expert judgement and insightful comments, and congratulations to these brilliant writers. We're pleased to be able to bring you three of these fine stories.

Rebecca Wurtz is the author of County, Kind of a Love Story *(Nine Bean Rows Press), a novel in verse, and she was a runner up in the 2015 Texas Observer* Short Story Contest *with 'Hands moving through hair'. She lives in Minneapolis and teaches at the University of Minnesota School of Public Health. A transplant surgeon once told her about a program that was cancelled for the reasons described in 'Xuefei and his heart', and she wondered what became of the heart.*

XUEFEI AND HIS HEART

BY REBECCA WURTZ

Xuefei sat on a metal stool in the corner of the operating theatre. He'd been awake all night, and now, sitting in the quiet of the deserted room, he felt drowsy. He had transported the heart of the criminal executed at dawn from the prison infirmary to the university hospital's surgical suite, built especially for this demonstration. American transplant surgeons, collaborating with Chinese colleagues, were scheduled to do the first heart transplant on Chinese soil.

The murky green of the theatre calmed Xuefei after his frantic cross-town ride. The taxi driver wanted to charge extra because of the heart, and Xuefei had argued in the morning twilight, finally tipping him a coin.

Tap tap tap. A sound was coming from the metal bucket in

which the heart floated in electrolyte solution. Tap tap. Xuefei was surprised and approached cautiously. Tap! He jumped back; then, gathering his wits, he lifted the lid, just the width of his thumb. A voice inside spoke.

What's the hold up? asked the heart, peevishly. Why haven't I been transplanted? They promised I'd be placed into the chest of a high-ranking official.

"I don't know," Xuefei answered truthfully. "I fell asleep. I'm just the courier." The gatepost to his *hutong* sometimes muttered disgusting nonsense to him. The live scorpions, writhing on skewers at the market as they waited to be deep-fat fried—they shrieked in tiny voices, begging him for mercy. But he had never talked to the heart of a criminal. He wondered what the wicked man had done.

"Do you mind if I ask? What crime did you commit?"

Oh, I'm an evil heart. I caught my mistress with another man. I found them in his butcher shop, and I used his cleaver—are you sure you want to hear this?

"No!" Xuefei said. "Yes," he breathed.

The heart described how he dismembered the butcher, hanging the body parts on meat hooks with the pig carcasses in the window.

I was sentenced to death. But I could redeem my reputation by donating my organs. That, and the prison guards beat me until I agreed.

Xuefei felt faint and had to sit on the stool. After a few minutes, he approached the bucket again.

"Where did your other organs go?"

A kidney is going to a provincial deputy governor. The liver is travelling to Macau for the president of a casino.

Xuefei remembered hearing these plans from the other couriers in the waiting room.

And the brain, well, the brain is splatted against the brick wall at the prison.

An old woman, dressed in operating room garb, pushed a wide wet mop into the room. She was surprised to see Xuefei. "What are you doing here?"

Xuefei dropped the lid closed. "Waiting for the surgeons," he answered carefully.

"Don't you know? The procedure was cancelled. When the Americans heard the donor was a prisoner, they got squeamish. Everyone's gone home." She swiped her mop around the room and back out into the hall.

The heart tappity tapped against the metal.

Xuefei, this is a bad turn of events.

"I'm not going to be paid—"

Not that! I am a heart without a body.

"Oh."

You seem like a smart fellow.

"I *am* a smart fellow."

Take me home. Hide me under the sink in the washroom.

"I don't think I can. My mother and I share the toilet with the Lius, the Dengs, and the Yangs. Mrs Yang keeps the tub in which she soaks her feet under the sink, and—"

All right! Hide me in your clothes cupboard.

"My clothes cupboard?"

No, Mrs Yang's clothes cupboard. Of course *your* cupboard, idiot! Next, call my mistress.

"She's still your mistress after you murdered her boyfriend?"

We reconciled during my trial. She's a clever girl and will figure something out.

Xuefei felt a pang of envy. This criminal, or his heart at least, had a girlfriend, whilst he, a hard-working courier, had never been with a woman.

I buried the kickbacks I received as an official in the courtyard of her apartment block. The combination for the strongbox is 14-08-82. Can you remember that?

"Of course," said Xuefei. "That's my birth date. In the Year of the Dog."

Not an auspicious year, Xuefei.

Xuefei was beginning not to like this heart. It was bossy and insulting.

He had a few *yuan* left from the taxi fare, so he stopped in a tavern on his way home. The tables were occupied with workmen drinking beer and smoking cigarettes. Xuefei put the bucket on a stool at the bar and climbed up next to it.

Why are we stopping? hissed the heart.

"I haven't had breakfast."

Dummy! I can't last in this bucket forever.

Xuefei's feelings were hurt. "We won't stay long." He ordered a beer with a *baijiu* chaser.

You know, the only reason you have that courier job is because your mother bribed the hospital administrator.

Xuefei ordered another beer.

You drink too much, Xuefei, and you have unclean thoughts. You touched the little Deng girl when you found her in the toilet.

"She didn't tell anyone."

When are . . . when are we going . . . home? The heart seemed sleepy and dull, even a little drunk.

Xuefei had enough money for three beers and another *baijiu* chaser with a few *jiao* left over.

The heart started to snore.

A barman shook Xuefei awake. "Time to hit the road, buddy."

He staggered home, stopping at the food stall to buy a bundle of spring onions and a block of bean curd. The heart slept; the scorpions and gatepost were silent.

That evening, Xuefei's mother happily lifted pieces of stir fry to her mouth. "Son, you have made a very fine dinner. How was work last night?"

"I was given an important job, and I carried it out perfectly."

"I will tell *that* to Mrs Yang the next time she says you are a good-for-nothing. Beef heart, you say?"

"Yes, Mother. With green onions and bean curd."

Jenna Park is the flash fiction editor for the Denver-based literary magazine Gambling the Aisle. *She currently resides in Los Angeles, where she is an MFA candidate at Loyola Marymount for Writing and Producing for Television. Her work has appeared in* Connotation Press: An Online Artifact, Eunoia Review, Black Mirror Magazine, *and several times on her mother's refrigerator.*

$\mathscr{P}$AINTED NAILS

BY JENNA PARK

I don't know this house as a home but it smells like Christmas in the bathroom, even in June, because we only moved in six months ago and we'll leave before the trees turn orange, before my two older sisters go back to the high school, much cooler and prettier after the summer than the two months off changed me. Which is to say that I look the same, no taller, the only girl returning who still looks like a child, in the same clothes I had on the last day of fourth grade, worn, with grass stains on my knees that are the source of so much contention between my mother and my father.

My mother tells me to have patience when she buys my sisters new clothes, because high schoolers can be so cruel and children still have manners and haven't learned to be mean yet. By this time, I know how wrong my parents can be but haven't yet developed the courage to argue.

While my mom sorts through the bills my dad feeds us too much ice cream , trying to overpower the loudness of being poor with banana splits he made himself, even though my oldest sister tells him how much she hates bananas and this new house, and how much she will hate the next one even though we haven't picked it yet. And I hate my sisters for making my mom roll her eyes, for making my dad wash so much ice cream down the sink. And I hate this house for smelling like Christmas when there won't be snow for ages, and I hate Christmas because no matter how much I try to pretend I'm not expecting anything, I always feel disappointed, and my older sister (but not the oldest) tells me not to be such a child.

The day before school starts my mother takes us out, just us girls, to get our nails done, our end-of-the-summer ritual, and we all fight in the car, another ritual, and my sister says she doesn't even know why we're going if we can't afford it. My mother turns up the radio to drown us out, but over the music I hear her say, We always have enough money to be beautiful.

We let the ladies paint our nails, and my sisters don't pick on me, and we don't worry about the money or the clothes. And I'm no longer a child, the red I chose bold on my fingertips and toes, but a woman.

The next morning, I slam my finger on the counter and chip the polish off my pointer, my most prominent finger. My older sister helps me peel the rest of the paint off, and we both cry as the smell of alcohol stains our faces, pretending we don't notice each other in this house that is a stranger.

__Anna Belkine__ is a data analyst, living in California. She writes during those powerful moments of creative inspiration that occur when both of her kids are asleep at the same time. Her flash fiction story, 'The Ravens' came out in Pulp Literature *Issue 6, Spring 2015, and we're delighted to be able to print a second piece by her. This story was penned during the Creative Ink Festival 2016 in Burnaby, BC, when, emboldened by the horror fiction panel, the author decided to take a stab at the genre.*

$\mathcal{B}$etter Watch Out

by Anna Belkine

Sally and I were terrified of Santa as children. No, not those impostors who hung around shopping malls. The real Santa lived in our air conditioning vent. You could hear him moving in there, every once in awhile—a sort of wet rustle. We knew our parents could hear it too, but they tried very hard to be dismissive about it. This was just the sound old vents made in the winter, they said. Santa was just a myth, they said. But the terror in their eyes told me he was real. They *knew* he was real. That he was there. And they were *lying*.

He came out only when we slept. Somehow he could always tell if we were just pretending. Like in the song. You would hear him come out just as you felt your body go limp, just as your consciousness slipped heavily out of your belly and you were no longer able to command your eyes to open. You could feel him, moving around the room, the large round mass of him, dressed in the sort of shimmering red hues that creep behind your eyelids on bright days. And he talked, a lot, all the time, using mangled sounds neither pronounceable nor reproducible. All we understood at first was that his name was Santa. The way he said it, it sounded like a heavy scuffling, followed by the noise of something viscous dripping heavily on a linoleum floor. Sssss— tah. Tah. Tah.

We had no choice but to listen to him scuffling and hovering and looming there in the dark, behind our closed eyelids. He never threatened. He was just waiting. For the opportunity to be mean. And we were waiting too, immobilized by sleep, like insects under a pane of glass.

Some nights, we could make some excuse not to sleep in our beds. Some nights we managed to stay awake until morning. But in the end, we were still made to lie in the dark by ourselves, with him behind the vent. *Rustling.* Eventually we understood that it was important to our parents that we do that. They *let* him visit us. That must have been the deal they made with him. Sally and I were on our own.

Especially Sally. See, I was the favourite child. Our parents made a token effort to conceal it, but it wasn't enough; we both knew it, we both felt it. She was in their way. An embarrassment. It's not like they actively *wished* her gone, no — but it was clear they would have been relieved if she were. Just as I could feel the evil skulking around in our room, I could feel her loneliness and her rejection clinging to me, a skinny bundle of ribs, knees, and gasps. Without me, she had nobody.

Christmas was the worst. He'd begin visiting nightly starting around the end of November, dripping wet terror on our floor. Sssss— tah. Tah. Tah. Eventually we started making out his words better, and he told us about the cookies. How he *needed* them, how we *had* to make them—cookies and milk; exactly six cookies on a white plate and mulled milk in a red cup, left on a white crocheted doily. They were easy enough to make, but we had to do it ourselves, in secret.

I wanted to tell others about it at first. Sally was against it—she thought talking to grown-ups always made things worse. Sally was right. Our parents were in on it. They just said it was *adorable,* cookies for Santa. Ain't that precious, haw haw. We wised up after that.

The Easy-Bake Oven was sufficient for our purposes. We baked them in our room, behind closed doors. Tollhouse chocolate chips, flour, butter, and half an ounce of blood from each of us. An ounce was however much fit in a shot glass. But you could never get enough of it from just a pricked finger: the wound would close up too early, and blood dripped too slowly. After a hockey injury, I found out that the best place to bleed was the scalp, under the hairline. Easier to conceal the wound, and easier to direct the flow. It just dripped down a lock of your hair, into the glass. Heavy viscous drops. Bright red. Tah. Tah. Tah.

'Twas the night before Christmas. When we came upstairs, our parents were there, in our room. Sally froze in place and went pale. They had been angry at her for days, for something she did, but she never expected them to do this to her. "Those were for Santa ..." she said. But they didn't respond. Just carried the empty plate right past her. "You're grown up now," mom said. "Time to learn how things really work."

We sat on the bed that night, facing each other. Awake. Waiting. Our parents snoring downstairs. No chance we'd fall asleep, not a chance. We thought that maybe if we just stayed awake, that Santa wouldn't come. But then we felt the snoring stop. There was a wet rustle. Sssss ... Wet, red, viscous dripping sound. Closer and closer. Sssss— tah. Tah. Tah.

I don't know how my parents covered it up. Maybe they knew somebody. All I know is that after finding me the next morning they shipped me upstate for four months, and then after I came back, it was like she was never there. They changed the wallpaper and the carpet upstairs—as if it could make me forget what happened. What they *made happen*. They called this "moving forward." The essence of it was to try and make me feel the same relief they were feeling at Sally being gone. I didn't buy it.

I guess there was one thing that was a relief. Santa went quiet. So quiet that some days I even forgot about him. He never asked for cookies anymore. He still rustled occasionally, around Christmas, but it was a *sated* rustle. Fat. Jolly. Sssss ... tah-tah-tah.

IT RAINED THEN TOO

Anat Rabkin

"Love is three parts hard work and one part sacrifice," says Vancouver writer and illustrator **Anat Rabkin**, whose story 'Forbidden Fruit' appeared in Issue 9 of Pulp Literature. "This time I wanted to tell a down-to-earth story, of two people struggling through life and love and figuring out each other as well as themselves." For more from Anat, including her beautiful webcomic Seraphim, go to lunarblade.com or patreon.com/seraphim.

YEAH,
IT'S SHOWING AT
THE VIP CINEMA ON
FRIDAY. WANNA
GO?

ADRIAN?

NATHANIEL?!

WHAT THE
HELL ARE *YOU*
DOING HERE?

I
THOUGHT YOU
WERE BACK
EAST?

BRRING!
BRR—
BZZT
BZZT—
BRRING!
BRRING!
BRRING!
BRRING!
SORRY!
SORRY.

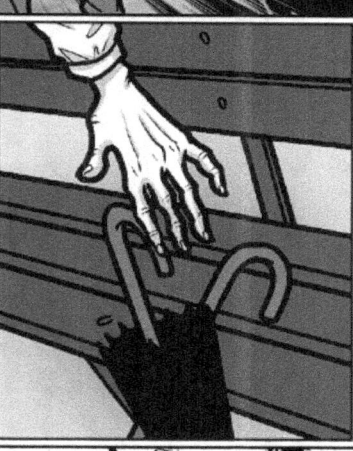

THIS IS YOUR BUS, ISN'T IT? IT'LL TAKE YOU TO THE THEATRE.

SCREW THE MOVIE. YOU'RE BACK.

YOU'RE BACK.

I'M SORRY. I WAS BEING AN ASS.

I'M HERE.

I'M BACK.

I'VE MISSED YOU SO MUCH.

ALLAIGNA'S SONG: ARIA

JM Landels

Aria is the second novel in the Allaigna's Song *trilogy by equestrian swordswoman, artist, and editor* **JM Landels**. *The first book,* Overture, *was printed serially in issues 1 through 11 of* Pulp Literature, *and will be available in a single volume from Pulp Literature Press in early 2017. This book picks up where* Allaigna's Song: Overture *left off.*

*I*N ALLAIGNA'S SONG: OVERTURE . . .

Fourteen-year-old **Allaigna** discovered that her family lied to her all her life: that her nurse Angeley is really her grandmother and former Princess High of Brandishear; that Allaigna herself is the product of a tryst that occurred when her mother was lost in the Valnirata Greatwood en route to her marriage. Fuelled by hurt and anger, Allaigna stole her mother's only keepsake of the man who rescued her — his Ilvan dagger — and fled from her home and her unwanted betrothal, hoping to find her father by retracing her mother's decade-and-a-half-old route.

Former Princess High **Irdaign**, once set aside and separated from her daughter, used her power of the Sight to tweak the strings of fate. She returned to her former calling as a midwife, arriving in Teillai in time to aid the birth of her granddaughter, Allaigna.

Lauresa of Brandishear found love for the first time in the unlikely aspect of the wanderer who saved her life on the Clearwater road. But staying with him and forsaking her intended marriage to the Duke of Teillai would have meant war between the Ilvani of the Valnirata and the four principalities of the Ilmar. Duty overcame desire, and she arrived for her wedding not yet knowing she carried her lover's child.

Verse I

Blood and Guts

Heroism is not in my bones. It is in my blood, certainly. My mother, my father, my grandmother and grandfather: all of them have made heroic sacrifices, taken courageous leaps of faith, risked their hearts and lives for the greater good, or thrown themselves between others and their fates. Some have even made a profession of it.

When I ran away from my home at the age of fourteen, determined to find my birth father and wounded to the quick by the lies my family had told all my life, I was being brave—though foolhardy may be the better term—but not heroic. Heroism would have entailed staying where I was, working with my mother and grandmother, and even accepting the hand of Tiern Doniver for the good of Aerach. Instead I left a string of diplomatic incidents, and a trail of blood, in my fleeing wake.

My only defence for the havoc I created in my selfish angst is temporary insanity. I was, after all, fourteen.

By the time the sun was halfway to its midpoint on the first day of my hasty flight from Teillai I realized my error and changed direction. Searching for my father by retracing the route he and my mother took fifteen years ago had a romantic sort of logic, but the road to Werrancross was far too populated for the daughter of the Duke on the run from her betrothal. Several times already I had been seen, and perhaps even noticed. For who wouldn't notice a lone sliver of a girl astride an over-tall, raw-boned gelding, pounding the road in the early light of dawn? So I took leave of the road at the next crossing and spent a few hours slogging through hedge-lined irrigation canals. I meted out the rest of the day along country lanes, losing the morning's gains in a zigzag path eastward. By nightfall, my seat bones were raw, my knees were locked stiff, and I laid out my bedroll in the Eastern Forest only a few leagues from where I'd started.

The temptation to turn tail and run home like a chastened hound was strong that night.

The second day ground my seat bones further through my flesh, rubbed the top layer of skin away from the inside of my knees, and made my ankles creak and protest every time I dismounted to lead Nag through thick undergrowth and tangled roots. The sun remained cloistered behind pale, cold clouds, and I judged my direction only by the moss on the trees. At the end of daylight, still less than twenty leagues away from Teillai, I wondered what was worse: being found and dragged ignominiously home by my father's—no, not my father's, the Duke's—rangers; or never being found at all.

The urge to run home the second night was tempered by the small increase in distance and my greater uncertainty that I could even find home.

The third morning I hobbled about like an old woman, shivering and packing up bedding that had been drenched by an icy overnight rain. I dreaded settling in the saddle, sure there was no more flesh left between my bones and my breeks. My voice was thick with cold and disuse, nearly as creaky as my bones, but I sang as I groomed Nag nonetheless.

My body warmed and loosened with the effort of grooming, and so did my voice, the notes finally coming pure and resonant, vibrating between the dandy brush and my horse's sides, filling the air with the Leisanmira magic that was my birthright. I had tried this small charm yesterday, but had only succeeded in a mild scorching of Nag's thick black winter coat, making him look as if he had faded in the sun or lain in a manure pile too long. Today, though, I found the right notes, the right sequence. With rhythmic strokes I brushed the black out of his hair, turning his flanks a ruddy bay.

I stood back to assess the effect. Granted, the pink light of the morning sun heightened the red, but even in the shade his coat was a definite russet brown now. It would be better to continue on his mane and tail, turning him chestnut, but perhaps I would leave that till tomorrow. I had no idea how long the colour change my song had wrought would last; I might have to repeat this every day. A different horse each day would go a long way toward throwing off any pursuit, and I wondered how much effort it would take to turn him dun, or grey, or skewbald. It was tempting to try it on myself as well: to go from black hair to blonde, and pale skin to tanned; but with no mirror I thought it best not to make the attempt. Instead, I used the curved cruel blade of my father's—my true father's—dagger to hack off great hanks of my long, dark hair. I hid the remaining hair beneath a woollen cap and hoped it was disguise enough.

As I tucked the dagger back into my boot, Nag's head shot up, ears pricked. He didn't snort, which meant he thought whatever it was was dangerous. If it were other horses he would have whinnied a greeting. But for a deer, or bird, or other harmless creature he would have snorted to let me know all was well after the initial alert. That he was still frozen, silent, nostrils flaring and muscles tensed to flee, meant it was likely a predator.

My throat went dry and sticky as I turned to scan the surrounding trees and bushes. Nag flicked an ear at me. He was not yet saddled or bridled. I considered fleeing the invisible threat bareback with just a halter, but getting onto Nag's tall back without stirrups or a stump to stand on was beyond me. I cursed my arrogance in not keeping the beautiful grey pony my father — the Duke, I mean — had given me. That pony I could have mounted bareback. That pony, though no warhorse, was trained to seat and voice commands. That pony was a mare, and thus more likely to defend a fallen rider.

I forced my brain to stop rattling and focus. The forest was almost silent. Not even birds or squirrels rustled or chirped. But there was a distant disturbance, like a windstorm coming closer.

Nag's already tight-wound nerves got the better of him. He bolted, crashing into the undergrowth. I dived for my packs, drawing out my thin Ilvani sword and wishing it were a spear. The thrashing of undergrowth was in both ears now: the sound of Nag's retreat growing fainter, and the other growing louder. Somehow I knew it would be a boar, even before its maddened red eyes and blood-streaked shoulders burst from the bushes. The broken haft of a spear protruded from its thick neck.

The pain-mad creature hurtled at me, and the years of drills with Baredh, Rhiadne, and Edris took over my body. I stepped sideways with a calm I didn't know I possessed, and drove my sword, two-handed, into the beast's neck. It skewered itself with its own momentum, driving the pommel out of my hands and into my belly. The blow collapsed my knees, and the boar finished the job, smashing me to the ground as it tumbled forward.

I lay there for several whistling breaths, listening for the inevitable hounds and riders that would surely discover me. I am not sure if I was disappointed or relieved when none came. At last I sat up, retched, and fell back again clutching my stomach. When I did manage to right myself I spotted the boar, half a dozen paces away. Its sides were heaving, but it was otherwise immobile. My sword was stuck in its neck like a great carving knife, the hilt waving gently with each of the pig's ragged breaths.

If I sat there long enough, would the boar die? I hardly saw how it could live with a both spear and sword inside it. But what if it were just winded, and then recovered enough to get up and attack? Or run away … with my sword?

I stood, shaking, grasping the trunk of a nearby tree. The boar gave a feeble twitch of its feet and tried to raise its head. That's when I noticed how small the tusks were. And the belly, now exposed to me, sported a double row of milk-filled teats. Not a boar: a sow.

A warm rush of anger made me forget my bruises. A sow! What sort of mould-rotted conscience would let someone hunt a sow, especially at this time of the year, with piglets in the nest?

I sidled around her, keeping well away, terrified she would surge to her feet and charge again. Her eye followed me but she didn't, or perhaps couldn't, move. She would die if left, a long slow death. Noise had returned to the forest, including the commentary of a pair of crows perched above us, waiting.

I slid the dagger out of its place in my boot-top. It had once belonged to the father I'd never met. I'd stolen it from my mother before slipping away like a thief in the night. Like my sword, it was Ilvani-made, but far crueller and uglier, with its dark curved handle and blue-black hooked blade. It was sharp, though, and would pierce a wild pig's tough hide better than my hunting knife.

Continuing my sideways circle behind the sow, I rehearsed in my head what I needed to do. She scrabbled in the leaf mould with her sharp toes when I crossed into her field of vision. I took in a breath that sounded nearly as ragged as hers, forcing my heart to calm and my hands to still. With my second breath I lunged, grasping the hilt of my sword in one hand to hold the poor skewered creature still and drew the sharp steel of the dagger across her throat.

Blood fountained as the sow convulsed and rolled; I had to jump backward or be knocked over. Then she lay still, except for the slow pulses of blood draining into the forest floor.

My legs and hands were spattered with red. Unthinking, I put a knuckle in my mouth and sucked as if the drops of blood were my own. When I realized what I was doing, I spat, horrified. Then my stomach rumbled, reminding me I hadn't yet eaten. The supplies in my pack were already getting low, after only two days on the road. As much as I disliked meat, and the sight and smell of raw flesh especially, I had to admit that the sow's warm blood tasted little different than my own: salty, and really not so bad. There was a lot of food on those bones.

Wishing I'd packed small cords — one of the multitude of things I wished I'd packed — I pulled a leather lace out of my jerkin and used it to lash the sow's hind feet together. At least I had a sturdy rope, which I looped through the hind legs. Tossing the free end over a tree branch, I hoisted the pig off the ground. She was heavier than I, and I would not have managed it at all had I not sung a song, lessening the pull of gravity on her. Nonetheless, it cost a great deal of sweat and a number of rope-burns before I got her high enough to lash the end of the rope around the tree trunk and leave her swaying above the ground.

I widened the slash I'd already made in her throat and stood back, wrinkling my nose in revulsion while the rest of her veins and arteries drained. Angeley would have chided me for wasting the blood, but I had no hounds to feed, nor any way to make soup or pudding of it. Just because I'd stomached a drop of raw pig's blood did not mean I was about to add it to my diet.

The beautifully sharp Ilvani knife made easy work of the gutting. I could hear Angeley scold me again as the blue, dark intestines slithered to the ground. But I had no use for those either.

"All the more for you, friends," I said to the half-dozen crows watching me with patient intent.

When the sow was cleaned to my satisfaction I stood back, wiping my blood-drenched hands and knife on a clump of moss. A week ago, I would likely have thrown up at the mere thought of gutting a pig. Today, though I'd taken no pleasure in the task, I felt a gleam of pride in my own sufficiency.

However, I had no time for self-congratulation. I had a horse to catch.

A horse will flee thirty or so galloping strides before it slows and begins to curve its trajectory into a wide arc to see whether it has been followed. It strikes a balance between its need to run from danger and its need to conserve energy and keep the herd together. In a wooded area the flight is shorter, and it was at about fifty of my paces that I saw Nag's track veer east and lose its war-torn look. I angled off the track, scoring a tree-trunk now and then with my knife so as not to lose my way. When I calculated I was near enough, I whistled four short notes and a long one, as I did whenever I approached the paddocks at home with a carrot in my pocket.

Sure enough, I saw movement through the scrub and trees, and long ears pricking high above the bushes.

"Nag," I called softly, moving to a clearer patch of ground.

He came, picking his way over dead wood, his nostrils still showing a wary red, but glad enough of my company and the withered piece of carrot I offered him.

"Good boy, goooood boy," I crooned.

He shied away as I rubbed his forehead. The smell of blood must still have been strong on me, but I scratched his poll and breathed into his nostrils, reaffirming our understanding before leading him back to the mess of a campsite.

The morning was almost gone before I tacked up, cleaned up, and managed to sling the sow's carcass across Nag's protesting back. He danced like a racehorse, snorting and tossing his head, and I had to sing him near to sleep before he'd put up with it. It left me almost too tired to move, but I climbed into the saddle anyway, for I was fired with a new purpose.

Boar hunting is forbidden in the springtime.

I did a check of my mental map. Two days ago, I had left the Werrancross road before crossing the River Hunthad, and I'd traversed no rivers since. I was still west of the far edge of the Werran Forest, and that meant I was within the Duchy of Teillai and its laws. The penalty for hunting out of season was stiff. Hunting a sow incurred even larger fines, and perhaps a short term in prison for a nobleman. For a commoner, it would be stocks at the least, or perhaps a branding or the gallows.

While I did not want particularly to see anyone sent to the gallows, I was compelled to pursue justice: not on behalf of my erstwhile father, the Duke, but on behalf of the sow and her now motherless piglets. I had no idea what I planned to do when I found the perpetrators. The chances of me overpowering even one poacher, let alone a party of them, were nil. Nonetheless, I felt obliged to investigate.

The sow's trail was easy enough to follow backward, though I was surprised how far she'd come in her wounded state. Her track broke at last on the verge of forest and rangeland. At first I thought I would lose her trace as the ground became firmer and grassier, but then I saw hoof prints—more than one set—converge where the sow's path had originally left the woods. I dismounted and tied Nag to a tree to avoid further confusing the tracks. Though the prints were harder to see, there were traces of dog as well.

The story was easy enough to read for one who'd spent as many hours at Rhiadne's heels as I had. The horsemen, galloping along the forest verge, had met with the sow who had been driven from her den by hounds. A mix of hoof prints and bark rubbed from the trees showed where the horses had been tied. There had been no pursuit of the wounded sow, except by the hounds; but human boot prints led back into the woods the way the pig had come.

I followed them, and sure enough, they led to the sow's nest, farther back in the woods. There was a mess of human and canine prints where the dogs had rejoined their masters, but not a piglet to be found. No blood either, though plenty of crushed undergrowth showing busy activity. The hunters, it seemed, had left with a sack full of live piglets.

For what? To raise on goats' milk and fatten for the autumn? How a pen full of wild piglets would escape the notice of the bailiffs, I wasn't sure. But these were wealthy folk, for they had hounds and horses. Did they really need to poach newborn marcassins?

I jogged back to find Nag peaceably cropping new grass, having grown accustomed to the sow's carcass across his saddle. Once back aboard my grubby brown mount, I sent him off at a canter along the return tracks of the horses.

This sort of rashness, galloping headlong, full of fury and empty of plans, may be typical of many fourteen-year-olds, but it was not typical of me. My natural sense of caution reared up before long and I slowed Nag to a walk when the first spiral of smoke became visible. Soon I could hear dogs and voices ahead. I pulled up, baffled by my complete lack of a plan.

I left off the riders' tracks and circled toward higher ground. The woods here were scattered and open, but a dense stand of birches veiled in new green screened the rise. I searched my memory for maps I'd seen, trying to recall the name of the nearest hamlet. By my reckoning I was west of the city of Doniver. It was a name that made me shudder, being also the seat of my intended betrothed. The largest town nearby was Scrantree, south towards the Valnirata border. I called up those long-forgotten taxation maps Willits had made me study: there were no other settlements in this ward, aside from a few hamlets clustered along the river. There should be nothing here. No farms, no holds. Nothing but forest and rangeland for the game that belonged to Teillai. And yet, above the birches, the smoke from at least half a dozen fires coiled defiantly in the air.

Ride on, my inner voice told me. *What do you care if a band of poachers steals some of your father's game? He's nothing to you.*

No, I answered, *he's not. But it's a matter of morals, not ownership. There's no excuse for hunting in the spring.*

The most logical course would be to report them to the sheriff in Scrantree, if it had a sheriff, or at least a bailiff or reeve. And if not Scrantree, then Doniver. But the thought of Doniver called up my parents' promise to its younger lord and some of the reasons I'd left home. Would they have notified old Doniver and his son of my truancy, or were they hoping I'd return quietly, with no one the wiser? They must have sent riders out in all directions. Or did the embarrassment of having a runaway daughter curtail any public search? Were they even—I stopped that thought before it went farther. Of course they were looking, and therefore I could not make contact with the authorities of any town, large or small.

The light of the short spring day was starting to dim, slivers of gold appearing at the edges of the western clouds. Dealing with the pig had taken half my day, and following her sad trail the other half. My stomach growled. I could not start a fire and cook some of her carcass here on the hilltop without alerting those below. And to go walking into their camp with the evidence of their crime slung across my saddle would invite scrutiny and hostility both. Besides, a girl on her own risked much, despite Teillai's harsh view of rapists and molesters. Teillai also took a harsh view of poaching, and what good had that done the sow?

There was one profession safe from interference. I had hoped and counted upon it while packing my saddlebags in a rage three nights ago. The unwritten pact with the Leisanmira allows the nomadic people to travel freely, owing fealty to none and protected, if grudgingly, by all. It extends to any travelling entertainer, whether Ilmari, Ilvani, or true Leisanmira, and it is a pact of convenience as much as tradition, for the news such people carry is valuable. The written word is lost on much of the population, but songs can make a political career almost as quickly as a bard's tongue sharpened in anger or disdain can destroy it.

I slung the sow's carcass from a new tree then spent extra time and effort singing charms to clean the blood from my saddle and clothes. It left me even more exhausted than the efforts of the morning, and I hoped it would not drain my voice too much. I rested a while, eating a precious spoonful of honey from the jar I'd brought for medicinal use and drinking most of the water in my flask. Once I felt refreshed I began to softly warm my throat with a few scales and ditties. It was far from its best, but it would have to do. I remounted Nag, steeled my nerves, and rode down into the valley under the blue clouds of dusk.

Lauresa's Chorus

Lauresa blinks, hardly believing it has stopped, that the burning pain is over. On her slack stomach, squirming wetly, is the child. Someone takes her hand, places it on the baby's back, then covers them both with a thick cloth. But no, she wants to see. Lauresa curls over, gathers the baby in both hands and lifts it—or her, for it is a girl—as high as the still-intact cord allows. The infant shivers, mewls in protest, and Lauresa pulls her close again, clutching the greasy, wet, and wrinkled creature beneath her breasts.

Tears start, and it is through these blurry curtains she gazes into the wise and searching eyes of her daughter. Here, in this moment, she could stay forever.

There is a voice beside her, both soothing and annoying, reminding her to push out the afterbirth. It is the midwife, but not the one with whom she began this long labour. Why does it seem like the nagging of her mother? She doesn't have a mother. Except Gwannyn. And Gwannyn never nags.

She finally tears her gaze away from the beautiful stare of her daughter, and is jolted by the face looking down at her. Fractured images like splinters of a broken looking glass stutter and shimmer at her, layering the midwife's face with long forgotten memories. She feels like throwing up again, though her stomach was empty long ago. She closes her eyes, and the relief of not seeing is palpable.

They are alone at last, the tiny girl child firmly attached to her breast, those wondrous eyes closed in concentration as the babe works at drawing out scant drops of first milk. It hurts Lauresa—the ferocious toothless mouth feels like it is drawing blood, not milk—but she wouldn't stop it for the world.

All I need is here, Lauresa thinks. For the first time, for as long as she can remember, she feels entire. This child completes her, makes her whole. Whatever lacks or wants she may have had, whatever losses or sorrows, they are irrelevant now. Even

Einavar, whose face has haunted her each day and night for the past nine clearmoons, has suddenly slipped back to a pleasant but distant memory. Instead there is Allaigna's face: there when she looks down at it; still there when she closes her eyes. She wants nothing more.

The sound of the chamber door opening disturbs her reverie. Irritated, she wills the intruder away, but knows nonetheless that a face will appear from behind the bed curtains. She even knows which face it will be. She is strong. She can face anyone, anything, now.

The midwife, the new one, pulls aside the curtain and sets a cup of something steaming into Lauresa's free hand.

"Raspberry leaf," she says in a voice at once so strange and so familiar it makes Lauresa want to cry.

Perhaps she is not so strong after all. Instead she summons anger, looking in all the dark corners of her otherwise happy soul to find it. Her own voice, when it comes out at last, is a trembling mix of emotions, but it is as steady as she can make it.

"Thank you ... Mother."

That is all the anger she can summon for this face from the past. There will be recriminations of course, and long-heated discussions. But today, on her daughter's birth day, she won't voice them. She lets the pain dissolve for now. It is not gone, and it will precipitate again. But for today she chooses gratitude.

"Thank you," she repeats, "for being here."

Her mother blinks, surprised perhaps. There are tears in those blue eyes so like her own.

Irdaign reaches out, touches Lauresa's hand, then her hair, her cheek. As if reassuring herself she really does exist.

"Oh, Lauresa, how could I not be?"

You were not for so much more of my life, Lauresa thinks.

Irdaign wipes her eyes on the rough sleeve of her dress. More of Lauresa's memories pour back, sending her stomach reeling again. So many little things. Her mother gathering herbs in the kitchen garden at the Bastion, those same sun-browned hands plumper, less spotted and veined, but just as strong and gentle, picking her up to straddle her hip. Standing regal in full court dress, accepting petitioners, running the castle, the town, the country, while Papa was at war. How could all of those scenes been forgotten so completely?

Irdaign leans over and pulls Lauresa and the baby together in an embrace.

"There is so very much to talk about, my love. But first, your husband would like to see you and his daughter."

Not his, thinks Lauresa, sure, as she had not been throughout the pregnancy.

"Does he know who you are?"

Irdaign shakes her head. "I think it's best he doesn't."

Lauresa nods agreement but sheds another inward tear for the new lie with which she anoints Allaigna's birth day. But it is a small one compared to the other.

"Send him in," she commands.

Allenis Andreg, Duke of Teillai, her husband, is as gruffly polite as he ever has been. As polite as he was at their betrothal. As polite and relieved as he was when she rode unaccompanied, two weeks late for her wedding and rather worse for wear, through the gates of Teillai. As polite and stately as he was on their hastily re-set wedding day, and as he was on their wedding night, when, if he noticed she was no virgin, he said nothing. As polite as he has been every day since then.

He took the improbable story of her adventure in the forest of the Valnirata at face value. Littered with truth, which was the most improbable aspect, it was as convincing a tale as she could make it. He did not question it, and assured her he would make no redress against the Valnirati, since it was their outlaws who had attacked her, and they themselves who had sheltered her. He expressed (polite) gratitude for her safe return, and then eschewed the matter (politely) to allow her to forget it.

Not so easy on her part.

Einavar's face haunted her sleeping and waking hours throughout the pregnancy. Andreg performed his conjugal duty on a metronomic schedule: every night for the first week of the marriage; every second night for the second week; then every third until it became evident Lauresa was with child. After that the Duke's appearances in the bedchamber ceased altogether.

Lauresa both desired and dreaded the encounters. She wondered if it would have been better or worse had not Einavar claimed her maidenhood already. On the one hand, Andreg's perfunctory mating habits may have seemed better without comparison to the heart stopping passion she had experienced with Einavar. On the other, at least she could close her eyes and pretend it was Einavar's long slim fingers that touched her, his thin and ropy-muscled body that lay across hers, his insatiable thirst for her that held them pinned together. It wasn't easy. Allenis and Einavar were as unalike as two men could be, but her imagination was strong. If she thought about the latter, recalled their passionate lovemaking in the Greatwood, she could work herself into a state of sufficient arousal so that, if she kept her eyes closed, at least it was not painful.

Allenis also performed with eyes closed. He arrived at her door fully ready, and slept or left immediately afterwards, as if his mind too was elsewhere.

And now … Now Lauresa's mind is somewhere completely new. The unlikely glimpses of Einavar's face she sees in the chubby features of Allaigna become less and less frequent, until all she sees is the baby girl herself. It is as if the gift of a child sprang from her body by magic. To her it is irrelevant that the babe is not Andreg's and that he seems so much less enamoured of her than Lauresa is. She is blissful simply ensconced in her bed with Allaigna nestled under her arm or latched happily on her breast.

It does not last long, this bubble of bliss. By the end of the second day the milk comes in, finally leaving the child content and sleeping for more than an hour. By the third day the tears come in as well.

Though Allaigna is still Lauresa's joy, she is her only joy. All else seems awash with bitterness, regret, and anger. Her memories, doctored away behind the spells of her father's mages, now break free and surge forth in tidal waves of feeling. Everything makes her want to cry, from minor adolescent angst she had all but forgotten, to her bittersweet fortnight with Einavar, to the heart-rending, soul-quelling betrayal of her mother's departure from her life. Even the happy memories—those from before her mother left her—cause bursts of tears, both of happiness and of bitter contrast to the rest of her life.

Her ladies in waiting, her husband, and the maids who sweep the fireplace all urge her to pass the babe to a wet nurse, to allow herself some sleep and a break from the child who obviously has tired her so. Only her mother, the woman who calls herself

Angeley, insists otherwise. And despite the weight of all those other voices, despite the furious, bitter anger coiled in her chest, she finds that, in this raw and vulnerable state, she is incapable of not listening to her mother. So she keeps the baby with her, nurses her from her own breast, and is grateful to do so. She obediently opens her mouth and lets Angeley place a small chunk of the afterbirth under her tongue as proof against the tears. Whether it is gipsy magic or superstition, she does feel better the following day and willingly accepts the treatment again.

Gradually, like clouds clearing, she reaches a state of near equilibrium: not the rapturous incapacitating joy of those first two days, but not the crippling sorrow either.

It has been a turn and a half of the clearmoon. The midwinter feast has come and gone, the ashes have been cleared from the great fireplace, and the household is busy cleaning the remains of festivity from the wide stone halls of Osthegn. Lauresa takes a deep breath, enjoying the crisp winter air sweeping through the rooms as the maids open shutters and shake out drapery.

Allaigna has fallen asleep at the breast, a dribble of milk flowing down her fat cheeks. Lauresa heaves herself out of the deep chair, pausing to rock the baby before walking softly to the canopied bed the two of them share. She sets the babe down in the middle and covers her with a small embroidered blanket.

It is one Irdaign brought with her when she arrived for Allaigna's birth, but it is more familiar than that. Memories of her childhood are so soft and inconsistent they melt like fog when she tries to touch one. But this she can touch ... and remember. The pictures in her mind are like paintings: static in their time, but immense in detail if she traverses them with her mind's eye.

It is there, crumpled at the foot of the small daybed in the solar, sun shining on it, dust motes weaving a pattern above it. Her small-nailed, pudgy child's feet press against the nubbly raised texture of the embroidery, tracing the patterns of leaves, flowers, and stars. Now she does this with her adult fingers, in the cold, dim, winter light. The still form beneath the blanket is not one of her wooden dolls with its beautiful painted wax face, but her own infinitely more beautiful daughter, with skin more pale and translucent, lips more delicate. A pinkish-mauve tinge finer than the finest tints on the royal dollmakers' palettes rests on those cheeks, beneath eyelashes thick, dark, and curved in sweet smiles below the barely-there line of brow. She remembers the doll, her favourite, which slept covered in this very blanket. She once thought she could love nothing so well or so much as that doll. But she has thought that about many things and people. Now she doesn't think. She knows.

§

Allaigna's Song: Aria *will continue in* Pulp Literature *Issue 14, Spring 2017.*

THE ARTISTS

ZORAN PEKOVIC
Cover artist, The Shadow
Zoran Pekovic is an illustrator, animator, commercial artist, and graphic designer based in sunny Montreal, Quebec, Canada. You can find more of his work at pekta.com.

MEL ANASTASIOU
In-house illustrator
Mel Anastasiou loves drawing for *Pulp Literature* because she loves the stories she illustrates. She draws in black and white, working from imagination and inspired by details from Renaissance compositions. You can find more illustrations, as well as writing tips and news about her books and novellas, at melanastasiou.wordpress.com.

ANAT RABKIN
Writer and artist, 'Forbidden Fruit'
Anat is the Vancouver-based artist-writer of *Seraphim: Tales of Love and Courage,* a twice-weekly webcomic (www.lunarblade.com). She loves movies, animation, books, comics, and tabletop roleplaying games, all of which give her inspiration to tell new stories. If she could pick one word to define herself, it would be *storyteller.*

JM LANDELS

Illustrator, Allaigna's Song: Overture

JM Landels studied at the Cartoon Centre in London, UK, under David Lloyd (*V for Vendetta*) and Dougie Braithwaite (*Punisher*). Although she is a perennial doodler, she put down her pencils and brushes after giving birth to three children, but rapidly dusted them off when she realized *Pulp Literature* was going to be an illustrated magazine. You can follow her on Twitter @jmlandels.

MARKETPLACE

Sydnye (Queen of the Universe) *by Scott Fitzgerald Gray*
When you're 13 life is complicated enough without finding out your dreams of shooting stars are real.
insaneangel.com

Tatterhood: Unwanted Visitors *by Kris Sayer*
Volume I of the graphic novel about a girl, her goat, and her wooden spoon.
tatterhood.com

Wedding Bands *by Ev Bishop*
Can a lost love truly be reclaimed?
evbishop.com

*B*OOKSTORES

Book Warehouse
632 W Broadway,
Vancouver BC
(604) 872-5711
bookwarehouse.ca

The Comicshop
3518 W 4th Ave,
Vancouver, BC
(604) 738-8122
thecomicshop.ca

Myth Hawker Travelling Bookstore
Canadian authors · Canadian content · small and independent press
mythhawker.com

Portrait of backer Carol McCauley's mother, by Mel Anastasiou.

CREATIVE INK
FESTIVAL

2017

March 31st - April 2nd

2017 Guests of Honour
We are thrilled to announce our Guests of Honour for the 2017
Creative Ink Festival!

Please give a thunderous applause for four time Aurora
Award winning author, Eileen Kernaghan as well as the award
winning, critically acclaimed author, Ken Scholes!

All events, all three days only $80

More information: http://creativeinkfestival.com/

Phoenix On Bowen
992 Dorman Rd,
Bowen Island, BC
(604) 947-2793

People's Co-op Bookstore
1391 Commercial Dr,
Vancouver, BC
(604) 253-6442
coopbks@telus.net

Regent Bookstore
5800 University Blvd,
Vancouver, BC
(604) 228-1820
regentbookstore.com

Village Books &
Coffeeshop
130-12031 First Ave,
Richmond, BC
(604) 272-6601
villagebooks@shaw.ca

White Dwarf/Dead Write
Books
3715 West 10th Ave,
Vancouver, BC
(604) 228-8223
whitedwarf@deadwrite.com

"Myth Hawker has a crush on the underdog: the small press, the overlooked author, the independent bookstore, and the vast, undiscovered treasures of small-scale publishing."

Myth Hawker travels the length & breadth of Canada, popping up at conventions & festivals in every province, showcasing the work of small press & independent Canadian authors. Follow them online to see where they're popping up next!

www.mythhawker.com   @Mythhawker

Conferences & Events

Creative Ink Festival · for writers, artists & readers
30 Mar 2016 — 2 Apr 2017, Burnaby, BC
creativeinkfestival.com

VCON 42 · Vancouver's original SF&F convention
October 2017
vcon.ca

Surrey International Writers' Conference
October 2017
siwc.ca

Magazines

Geist
Ideas + Culture · Made in Canada
geist.com

Mystery Weekly Magazine
The cutting edge of short mystery fiction
www.mysteryweekly.com

Neo-opsis
Canadian magazine of science fiction, based in Victoria BC
neo-opsis.ca

Polar Borealis
Paying market for new Canadian SF&F writers & artists
obirmagazine.ca/
polar-boreal-magazine

Room Magazine
Literature, Art, and Feminism
since 1975
Roommagazine.com

PRINTING & PUBLISHING
**First Choice Books / Victoria
Bindery**
Book Printing & Binding
Graphic Design · eBooks
Marketing Materials
1-800-957-0561
firstchoicebooks.ca

Wesbrook Bay Publishing
Beverley Boissery, author and
publisher
wesbrookbaybooks.com

CONTESTS

Pulp Literature runs four annual contests for poetry, flash fiction, and short stories. For contest guidelines, prizes, and entry fees, see pulpliterature.com/contests.

The Bumblebee Flash Fiction Contest

Contest opens: 1 January 2017
Deadline: 15 February 2017
Winner notified: 15 March 2017
Winner published: Issue 15, Summer 2017
Prize: $300

The Magpie Award for Poetry

Contest opens: 1 March 2017
Deadline: 15 April 2017
Winner notified: 15 May 2017
Winner published: Issue 16, Autumn 2017
Prize: $500

The Hummingbird Flash Fiction Prize

Contest opens: 1 May 2017
Deadline: 15 June 2017
Winner notified: 15 July 2017
Winner published: Issue 17, Winter 2018
Prize: $300

The Raven Short Story Contest

Contest opens: 1 September 2017
Deadline: 15 October 2017
Winner notified: 15 November 2017
Winner published: Issue 18, Spring 2018
Prize: $300

a paying SF and F market for beginning writers
issue 3 out now · free download

polarborealis.ca

STELLA RYMAN

and the Fairmount Manor Mysteries

Mel Anastasiou

ℬECOME A PATRON OF PULP LITERATURE!

Become a Patron of *Pulp Literature*

By supporting *Pulp Literature* on Patreon with $2 or more per month, you will be laying the foundation for a secure future for the magazine, as well as ensuring you will never miss an issue! Your subscription includes four big issues of short stories, novellas, poetry, comics, and novel excerpts, delivered to your door or or electronic mailbox each year.

Find us at patreon.com/pulplit

If you prefer to subscribe through our website, go to pulpliterature.com/subscribe.

Or you can send a cheque with form below to
Subscriptions, Pulp Literature Press, 8540 Elsmore Road, Richmond BC V7C 2A1, Canada

Don't miss an issue!

- ❏ **Send me 2 years (8 issues) at the special rate of $80** (save $40)*
- ❏ **Send me 1 year (4 issues) for $50** (save $10)*
- ❏ **Send me 2 years of digital issues for $30** (save $9.92)
- ❏ **Send me 1 year of digital issues for $17.50** (save $2.47)

Name: _____

Address: _____

City: _____ Prov. / State: _____

Postal code: _____ Country: _____

Email: _____

- ❏ Payment enclosed
- ❏ Bill me
- ❏ New
- ❏ Renewal

Make cheques payable in Canadian funds to S. Pieters. Include email address for digital editions and Paypal billing, or subscribe at www.pulpliterature.com.

*for postage outside Canada add $16 per year in North America or $32 per year overseas.